HER SECRET GARDEN

It seemed like a dream commission for landscaper Seren Evans — to restore a Victorian walled garden in Snowdonia for the famous model Chantrelle, as a surprise for her husband. But Seren soon finds herself trying to save the garden from Chantrelle's unrealistic attempts to create a tropical paradise in the wilds of Wales. Then, Chantrelle's rather attractive husband, Dylan, turns up unexpectedly and is furious at the 'destruction' of his beloved garden . . .

HEATHER PARDOE

HER SECRET GARDEN

Complete and Unabridged

LINFORD
Leicester

First published in Great Britain in 2003

First Linford Edition
published 2004

British Library CIP Data

Pardoe, Heather
    Her secret garden.—Large print ed.—
Linford romance library
    1. Gardens—Design—Fiction
    2. Love stories
    3. Large type books
    I. Title
    823.9′2 [F]

    ISBN 1–84395–567–9

Published by
F. A. Thorpe (Publishing)
Anstey, Leicestershire

Set by Words & Graphics Ltd.
Anstey, Leicestershire
Printed and bound in Great Britain by
T. J. International Ltd., Padstow, Cornwall

This book is printed on acid-free paper

1

'Hey, Seren, you didn't say it was a castle,' Matt Launston said as he stopped the battered little van in one of the few passing places on the single-track road that wound up the cliffs, and peered through the mist of a damp spring morning.

'Castle?'

The young woman in the passenger seat beside him looked up from her map with a frown.

'Alun didn't say anything about a castle. Are you sure this is the right road?'

'Well, you're the map reader, Miss Evans. I'm just following instructions,' he replied, his teasing grin crinkling the corners of his pale-blue eyes.

It was a look that, under normal circumstances, would have any woman within close range going weak at the knees. This time, the blue eyes opposite him were decidedly unimpressed. Either she knew him too well, or he was losing his touch, Matt thought to himself, ruefully. And, anyhow, he knew how nervous she was about this, the first time Alun had let them out on their own, without his guiding hand — definitely not a time to mess up.

He abandoned the charm, and gave her hand a quick, reassuring, squeeze instead.

'Maybe it's not a castle. It could just be a tower, a folly in the garden, even. Anyhow, it clearly said Haulfryn at the bottom of the hill, and we haven't passed any other road going off, so that has to be it.'

The oval face beside him relaxed a little. It had taken them longer than they had expected to get here, even though both of them were used to the narrow, winding roads of Snowdonia. They would only just make it on time, even if that was Haulfryn, and only a few minutes' drive away.

'You're right. It must be. Alun is so precise about things. It has to be.'

The next moment, the little van was roaming its way up the last few metres to the top of the cliffs.

'Precise? What was that you said about Alun being precise?' Alan asked a few minutes later.

'Well, at least it definitely is Haul-fryn,' Seren replied.

She dived into the bag at her feet, and pulled out a well-worn folder. The tall, iron gate in front of them had Haulfryn clearly woven into its Celtic twists and spirals. It was the rest of it Alun should have warned them about.

'So is that lot to keep people in, or out?'

Matt peered at the vast, stone wall stretching either side of the gate, until it vanished into the mist. Rolls of wire were stretched across the top, held in place by a row of vicious-looking spikes. As he spoke, a tall, stocky man of the bouncer variety, the kind you definitely would not wish to disagree with, was emerging from the gatehouse beside them.

'You don't suppose Alun has connections with the Mafia, do you?'

Despite herself, Seren giggled. The thought of their mild-mannered boss, with his elegant suits, and his passion for orchids, mixing with anyone remotely connected to concrete boots and knuckle-dusters, was too much for her.

'Well, people have been murdered over tulip bulbs in the past,' Matt retorted as he wound down the window of the van.

'Mr Launston and Miss Evans from Caradoc Designs,' he said, as broken-nose reached them. 'We've an appointment with Mr Lloyd for ten-thirty,' he added, holding up the letter Seren had retrieved from her folder.

Broken-nose scarcely glanced at the piece of paper.

'You're expected.'

He didn't seem in too much of a hurry to let them pass, though. He peered carefully round the van, shining the beam of a small torch around each fork and spade and secateur hung neatly along the walls.

'Any cameras?' he demanded, at last.

'Just my Polaroid,' Seren said, wondering what was going on.

'No cameras.'

A very solid-looking palm was held out, with the clearest of meaning. The two in the van looked at each other.

'Look,' Matt said, his usual good humour vanishing fast, 'we need that camera for our work. Didn't anyone tell you we're here on business? We're not a bunch of tourists, you know.'

'Camera.'

Broken-nose might as well not have heard a thing. The outstretched palm was still there, waiting.

'Oh, don't argue, Matt. I'm sure we'll sort it out with Mr Lloyd.'

Matt was showing signs of losing his temper, which was the last thing they needed. Seren smiled sweetly at broken-nose, and handed him her camera, but he ignored the smile.

'Follow the drive. Ring the bell on the green door at the side,' he muttered then returned inside the gatehouse, and immediately the iron gates swung open slowly to allow the van to make its way through.

'He's on the mobile, letting them know we're here, I expect,' Seren said, taking a glance back at him in her side-mirror.

'What, so they can get the cannons and the boiling oil ready?' Matt returned. 'I thought you said these were Alun's friends?'

'That's what he said on the phone. A favour for an old family friend, that's all he'd tell me.'

'Favour? Well, I hope they know that. And I'd like to know what they've got against cameras.'

'Oh, Matt, look!'

Broken nose and barbed-wire forgotten, Seren gasped as they turned a corner, and the trees opened up in front of them.

'It is a castle.'

Even Matt let go of his temper, and slowed the van.

'Not a real one. Victorian, I should say,' he added.

Victorian or not, Seren didn't care. Grassy banks stretched out all around them, surprisingly fresh and green for so early in the year. Ranks of snowdrops stood amongst the grass, their delicate white heads stirring gently in the breeze, intermingled with clumps of purple crocus, and brighter patches of yellow.

'It must be amazing when the daffodils are out,' Seren said, noting huge patches of stalks and leaves, each seemingly of a different variety, and stretching as far as the eye could see. Above it all, on the highest point of the hill, rose a single, round tower, dark against the sky, with the square outlines of battlements running all the way around the top.

Matt was impressed, Seren was sure of it. He couldn't quite hide the excitement in his eyes, which reflected her own.

'Alun did say it was a gift of a job,' she reminded him.

'There are gifts, and there are gifts,' Matt replied, drily, speeding up the van once more. 'I prefer mine without razor wire and ape-men butlers, thank you very much.'

'Butlers don't man gates, you idiot.'

'But they are always the one who did it, and that one has definitely done something. Murder at the very least, I shouldn't be surprised.'

'And when did you last see a film with a butler in it?'

'When did you last see one that didn't?'

More relaxed now, they squabbled happily over their differing tastes in large-screen entertainment, until they drew up into a wide, gravelled parking-space in front of the tower.

'They might at least have given it one more tower,' Matt remarked, as they stepped out of the van, and looked at the building in front of them. 'One seems a little mean.'

It was a strange-looking place. The rest of the castle was more like a house, on a large scale, admittedly. Like the tower, it was made of well-weathered stone, but, unlike the tower, it was rectangular in shape, and set with plenty of large windows, that would have looked just as much in place in a large, Victorian house. Battlements stretched across where the sloping roof of red tiles began, but, even to Seren's eyes, they looked less than convincing — toy battlements, playing at being a mediaeval fortress, rather than the real thing.

Wide, stone steps led up to the front entrance, which consisted of a pair of large, carved wooden doors inside an ornamental porch, supported by pillars which appeared to have escaped from some Greek temple.

'How to impress your friends and neighbours,' Matt said. 'I see that door is no shade of green I've ever known. It must be the tradesmen's entrance for us.'

'Over here.'

Seren had spotted the bright green door at the side of the house. They locked the van, swung their bags over their shoulders, and set off. The bell jangled and echoed inside. After a few minutes, footsteps could be heard making their way rapidly towards them. The door swung open, and a pretty young woman, no older than Seren, with a cheerful mass of auburn curls around her head, appeared.

'You found us then,' she said, smiling warmly. 'I knew Alun would give you good directions. Do come in. I'm Hefina Lloyd, by the way.'

Matt and Seren exchanged a quick glance. They had both been quite sure the letter making the appointment had come from a man. A Mr H. M. Lloyd, Manager. That is what it had said on the letter. Instinctively, Seren grasped at her folder once more. She found Hefina watching them, a glint of amusement in her eyes.

'My brother is expecting you,' she said.

The amusement spread over into her voice.

'I don't think this place is quite ready yet for a female manager. Might shake the battlements too much. Mind you,' she added to Seren, 'that doesn't mean to say we're not working on it.'

They followed Hefina along a seemingly endless network of passages. There were no windows, just bleak, fluorescent strips to light up the whitewashed walls. Closed doors appeared at regular intervals. At one point, they passed a row of old-fashioned bells, with the names of various rooms printed below them.

'This part used to be the servants' quarters,' Hefina explained. 'It can seem like a rabbit warren, at times, but you get used to it. At least the main offices are on the next floor, where there are windows. This is mainly storage, here. Very secure.'

And not a place to get lost in, Seren thought to herself. She wasn't normally claustrophobic, but the walls of the narrow passageway seemed to be pressing in on her. She hurried on, close behind Hefina. After a while, they went up a flight of steps. A small window allowed daylight in, and the fluorescent strips were replaced with ordinary bulbs under shades, which cast a gentler glow. Here, the walls were covered in framed water-colours and photographs. Seren dropped a little behind Matt and Hefina. She would have liked the time to linger a bit more, and take a closer look.

The water colours consisted mainly of landscapes — dramatic mountain scenes, ruined castles, and picture after picture of the changing moods of the sea. Even a fleeting glimpse revealed the painter to be no ordinary talent. The sea-scapes, particularly, were full of life and vigour, bringing each rock, each sea-bird straining against the storm, and each breaking wave so alive you could almost feel the salt-wind on your face.

It was strange, Seren thought, she didn't remember seeing any of them before, in a local exhibition, or as prints in the tourist shops, and yet, there was a familiarity about them, as if she had known them all her life.

'They are beautiful, aren't they?'

She discovered she had stopped without realising it in front of a storm battering a coastline, and Hefina had come back to join her.

'Stunning,' Seren agreed.

'I'd give anything for a talent like that,' Hefina said.

There was a sadness to her voice, almost as if she were mourning something that was lost for ever.

'Who — ' Seren began, but she was immediately interrupted by an exclamation from Matt.

'It can't be!'

He had walked ahead of the two women, and was standing in front of a photograph, which was positioned to attract the best of the light from the neighbouring window, and which seemed to reach almost from the ceiling to the floor. He turned eagerly to Hefina.

'Can it?'

A wry smile overtook Hefina's face. 'Probably,' she said.

When they caught up with him, Seren found Matt was staring at a photograph of a young woman. The photograph was the kind Seren had only seen in the pages of the more expensive magazines, and the young woman was stunningly beautiful, the kind who could turn heads just by walking down the street. Her slender body was draped in white silk, blown by some invisible wind to cling tightly around her. The same wind had set her long fair hair stirring like a halo around the delicate pallor of her face. She rested in a white glow of light, which gave a suggestion of surrounding her with cloud, or snow. The only striking colour in the entire portrait came from the intense sea-blue of her large, luminous eyes.

'That is Chantrelle, isn't it?' Matt demanded.

'Who?' Seren asked, and immediately

felt rather foolish.

'Chantrelle,' Matt said, as if she couldn't possibly not know.

'That certainly is Chantrelle,' Hefina said.

Seren looked at her quickly. Whoever Chantrelle might be, Hefina had no liking for her, of that Seren was quite sure. She could even detect a slight twist of bitterness marring the openness of their guide's pretty face. Hefina quickly put her inward thoughts aside, and looked at the two of them.

'Didn't Alun tell you?' she demanded. 'I know my brother asked him to be discreet, but not that discreet, surely.'

The blank look on both the faces in front of her was answer enough.

'It is Chantrelle who has employed you. That is why she went through Alun, rather than simply contact a local business. She knows Alun would never allow her privacy to be invaded. We have enough as it is with paparazzi at the gate every time they think she might be here.'

Matt was looking vaguely stunned. Seren didn't dare ask again just who Chantrelle was. Paparazzi meant someone very public indeed, the kind of someone who would want to guard their privacy with high walls, large amounts of razor wire, someone not to be argued with manning the gate, and a total ban on cameras.

'Oh,' she said, hoping she sounded suitably impressed.

There was no time for any further questions. Hefina was already knocking on a door next to the photograph, on which a brass plate read: **H. M. Lloyd, Manager**.

'Come in,' a voice inside said, a warm, masculine voice.

Hefina opened the door, and ushered the two inside.

'Huw will explain everything,' she said.

2

The office was small. There was only enough room for two desks, each of them dark and ornate, and with the appearance of being at least as old as the building. Through the panes of the sash window they could see the rolling lawns of a country estate, with the sea beyond, partly obscured by a line of wall and battlements.

Seren blinked. She was beginning to feel she had stepped into the middle of some costume drama. She would not have been in the least surprised if the man rising from behind the largest desk turned out to be wearing breeches and a cravat, and greeted them with a low bow. On the other hand, there was not a hint of dust or cobwebs anywhere, and the circling fish in the corner were not in any tank, but on the screen-saver of a patiently waiting computer. The manager himself was closing the lid of a decidedly state-of-the-art laptop, and emerged from behind the desk dressed in trousers and a well-worn sweater.

'Hello, pleased to meet you. Welcome to Haulfryn. I'm Huw.'

The manager appeared to be in his early thirties. His hair was lighter than his sister's, almost a reddish-gold in appearance, and with a touch of grey at the temples. Dark hazel eyes took in his visitors quickly. Whatever he made of them, nothing showed in the powerful lines of his face. A smile lit up his features as he held out his hand.

'You must be Seren.'

His grip was firm and strong, more that of someone used to hard, physical work rather than being stuck behind a computer all day.

'And Matthew,' he added turning to Matt.

'Matt.'

'Matt, take a seat. Tea? Coffee?'

It took a few moments for the details of the drinks to be sorted out, then Hefina disappeared, closing the door behind her.

'Sorry, we're late,' said Seren, glancing at the clock on the wall beside her.

Huw laughed.

'Don't worry, you're not at all late. We always allow at least half an hour for visitors to make their way up the drive, not to mention battling their way past John.'

No prizes for guessing who John might be.

'Sorry about your camera. House rules, I'm afraid. There are plenty of cameras here you can use, and yours will be returned to you when you leave, of course.'

'Thanks,' Seren said.

She'd half expected Matt to kick up a fuss about this, but since seeing the photograph of Chantrelle, he seemed not to mind at all. The one thing that was certain to disturb Matt's cheerful outlook on life was someone messing about with any of their equipment. Chantrelle must be someone very special for him to forget so easily the loss of their camera.

'Great place,' Matt remarked, looking around curiously.

'It is. I'd find it a bit isolated here, myself, especially in winter. Sometimes you can't get up or down that road for weeks, if it freezes. And even the helicopter can't make it, if it's really bad.'

Matt glanced at Seren.

'Helicopter,' he mouthed, silently and Seren returned a suitably impressed raising of her eyebrows.

Huw was leaning back to collect a file from his desk, but he glimpsed this exchange from the corner of his eye. He smiled inwardly. He had been wondering about them since they came through the door.

Partners, Alun had called them, getting ready to take over the business now he had finally decided to retire.

Huw had imagined the two would be

middle-aged at least to have achieved Alun's very exacting standards, and he was certain Alun, who could, in many ways, be rather old-fashioned, had meant partner strictly in the business sense of the world. Finding that Matt appeared to be his own age, and Seren a pretty young woman of twenty-five or so, he had naturally been curious, perhaps especially as the young woman was a particularly pretty young woman.

Funny, he mused, that Alun had not mentioned this fact. Alun was well-known for his eye for a good-looking female. In Haulfryn village, at the base of the cliffs, rumour went that his never having married was due to unrequited love for a local artist, famed almost as much for her looks as for her much sought-after paintings. Whether this was true or not, Huw had no means of telling. But he was aware that, even now, well into his sixties, Alun had never yet been seen without a beautiful woman on his arm.

Huw took a quick glance at Seren.

She looked Alun's type — blonde, bobbed hair, pale skin, lightly tanned, and those startling blue eyes that dominated the small, oval face. He was surprised he had never seen her with Alun, draped in silk, and swaying on high heels, being shepherded through a first night at the local theatre, a book launch, or the opening of some exhibition or other, the kind of social events Alun was never one to miss. On the other hand, she and Matt were sitting with the ease of two people who knew each other very well, and felt comfortable together.

Huw couldn't quite make it out. Still, they were likely to be working here for some months. There was plenty of time. He opened the folder, and smiled at them both.

'I expect you must be wondering what all this is about,' he said.

'Just a bit,' Matt said.

'Well, the idea is that it will be a surprise.'

Seren exchanged glances with her

companion once more. She wasn't sure she liked surprises.

'A surprise gift, that is.'

Seren winced. She definitely didn't like surprise gifts. Her mother was full of them. In Seren's experience, they usually consisted of the kind of dresses you wouldn't expect your grandmother to be seen dead in, or a blind date with a suitable young man. The young men were always perfectly nice, but Seren always just knew she would find herself hiding her yawns before the evening was half gone, despite all her mother's good intentions.

'What kind of gift?' she asked.

'A garden.'

She and Matt exchanged glances again. A garden? An entire garden? They had never even attempted anything so ambitious before, without Alun's guidance, and, given the size of the grounds, this was not likely to be some small patch of ground. To be in keeping with the place, it would have to be huge.

'It's all right.' Huw had seen their look. 'It's not going to be from scratch. The garden is already there, it's just been badly neglected for the past twenty years or so. The basic structure is in place. It just needs tidying up, plenty of pruning, and new planting. Chantrelle, Mrs Gruffydd, is quite clear about the kind of thing she wants. She's working in France for another three weeks, but she can be contacted by mobile and e-mail, and she has left a detailed plan for you.'

He handed over a large piece of paper. In the middle was the rough sketch of the garden. Pencils had been used to draw in blocks of colour. Details of the flowers and shrubs had been written in the space around, in small, elegant handwriting, with neat lines pointing back to the relevant shading.

'It's a walled garden!' Seren exclaimed.

Huw caught the barely suppressed delight in her voice, and smiled.

'That's right. It's the old kitchen garden. It would have produced most of the fruit and vegetables for the estate in Victorian times, even pineapples and peaches, so I'm told. It's in a sorry state now. It's time it was brought back to life.'

He rose to help his sister, who at this moment returned with the drinks.

'Don't you think, Hefina?'

'What was that?'

'The kitchen garden. High time it was brought back to life.'

There was a moment's pause. Seren looked up. Hefina was bending over mugs and spoons, as if they were the most important things in the world at this moment, but Seren caught the shadow passing briefly over her face. The next moment, the chestnut curls were swinging as Hefina straightened, and the cheerful smile was back.

'Of course,' she said, but she didn't quite meet the eyes of anyone in the room.

'So who is the surprise for?' Matt enquired.

He, too, had noticed the faint hesitation before Hefina answered.

'It's a wedding anniversary present,' Huw said, 'for Chantrelle's husband, naturally,' he added. 'The tabloids are quite right about that, at least. The Gruffydds are full of romantic gestures.'

A faint explosion, that might just have been a suppressed snort, escaped from his sister, although she made no further comment, and handed round the coffee mugs without a word.

'Isn't a garden transformation rather a difficult thing to hide?' Matt said, frowning as he peered over the plan once more.

'Ordinarily, but Chantrelle is a very determined woman, when she puts her mind to something. The anniversary isn't until May Day, and she has persuaded Dylan to take location work in the States until the week before. The plan is she'll meet him at Heathrow, and they'll arrive back on the morning of the anniversary itself. I have a feeling she's pulled in quite a few favours to get the timing right.'

Huw didn't just feel this, he knew it as sure as daylight, having personally worked his way through an extremely long list of telephone calls and e-mails. However, Chantrelle would not thank him for betraying her trust, so he kept his information as general as he could.

Matt's curiosity got the better of his manners. 'And what does he do?'

'Dylan? He's a photographer, a very well-known one, as it happens. The portrait of Chantrelle just outside the office is one of his, taken just a few weeks before they were married.'

'He is also a fine landscape painter,' Hefina added, quietly. 'The watercolours you were admiring, Seren, those are some of his.'

'Really?' Seren replied.

She found it hard to put together the glossy fashion shot of Chantrelle, which would not have looked out of place on the front cover of Vogue, with the stormy brush stokes of the sea-scapes.

'Of course.'

Something had fallen into place for Matt.

'I thought they looked familiar. I should have recognised the name.'

He turned to Seren.

'You should have spotted it, too. Your mother raves about him. She's got several of those storms in her living-room.'

'They must be prints, then,' Hefina said. 'He didn't sell many originals.'

Matt looked at Seren. She was staring down at the carpet, but he knew her well enough to realise that he was about to cause her serious embarrassment, and if he did, the squareness of her shoulders told him, she would not speak to him for at least a week. In her own quiet way, Seren could be surprisingly wilful, when she put her mind to something.

'I don't know,' he finished, lamely. 'Must be, then.'

He was rewarded by a smile, and a

warm look from those blue eyes that had his pulses racing, despite their promise to Alun not to even think about any involvement outside work, at least not until they had the business up and running and could afford for one of them to leave if it all went horribly wrong. It made sound business sense, of course, even though Seren's mother had roared with laughter at the time.

'You idiot,' she had told Alun. 'Even you should know that if you tell young people not to do something they'll immediately go and do it. Where would Romeo and Juliet have been if their families hadn't been fighting it out in the streets?'

'Nonsense. This is not at all the same.'

'Would you like to put money on that?' Seren's mother had replied, with a mischievous glint in her eye.

She knew full well that poor Alun would be shocked at the mere suggestion of gambling, and would refuse to answer, leaving her to win the argument.

All things considered, Matt and Seren had quietly agreed to stick to the rules, just to keep the peace, if nothing else. These last few months it had all worked very well. However, there was no time to think about this any further. They were finishing their drinks, and Huw was rifling in a drawer in one of the desks.

'There'll be a camera here, somewhere,' he said. 'Any particular kind?'

Matt looked at Seren.

'You choose. You're the artist.'

'Ha, ha,' Seren returned, good humouredly. 'I can just see my mug-shots of weeds making it into the Tate Modern. Straightforward as possible, please. Something that does everything for me. I'm not much of a photographer, I'm afraid.'

'This one OK?'

Huw pulled out a small silver object.

'It's got quite a good zoom, and it's digital, so you'll be able to download them on to the computer and print them out before you go.'

'Fine,' Seren replied, trying to sound as if she went digital every day of her life. 'They're only really like notes. It saves having to make a plan of everything.'

'Good.'

Huw handed her the camera with a smile.

'The battery's fully charged, so take as many as you like. Right, shall we go and see this garden, then?'

Matt and Seren followed him out of the door, through another long network of corridors, and out on to the rolling lawns of the garden. Hefina stayed behind, muttering something about work to be done.

'She's Dylan's secretary, sorry, personal assistant,' Huw explained, taking note of Seren's look of curiosity, and welcoming an excuse to start up a conversation. 'Looks after things this end, while he's away. She's done it for years, and he won't trust anyone else, so she's always run off her feet. She never seems to mind, though.'

'Oh,' Seren said.

She was beginning to see several reasons why Hefina might feel some resentment towards the beautiful young woman in the photograph.

'Have you worked here long?' she asked, feeling it might be wise to change the subject.

'Ten years, would you believe. Mind you, I've known this place all my life. Hefina and I were always here as kids. Dylan doesn't have any brothers or sisters, so we're more like family, really. That's why he trusts us to keep the place going, I expect. He can be a suspicious devil, at times.'

'Nice,' Matt muttered, under his breath.

This did not sound like an easy client to please. What with that, and Huw monopolising Seren's attention, he was beginning to have second thoughts about the entire project.

'This is Dylan Jones' family home

then?' he added, aloud.

'Yes. Been in the family for years. Each generation added bits, which is why it looks slightly strange. The saying in the village is that they were all as mad as hatters, but I think eccentric might be more accurate.'

'Great,' Matt said.

No wonder Alun had chosen not to discuss the details of the project with them. Matt was busily working out just how they could get out of this, and save face, when they followed a few steps down to where a wall was half hidden behind thick growth of laurel and rhododendron. Huw pushed open a red door, which squeaked loudly in protest, and they were through into the walled garden. The moment they stepped inside, Matt knew it was too late. He saw the look on Seren's face, and knew there was no way out.

'Oh, wow,' she breathed.

There were not many times Seren was lost for words. Now, she just stood and stared. She didn't know quite what she had expected — wilderness, maybe? The scene in front of her was certainly neglected. Brown remains of weeds and grass sprawled over paths, and patches of earth. A few saplings had begun to spring up between the frostbitten stems of thistles and giant teasels. In the very centre, a wooden construction of some kind had almost completely collapsed. Opposite them, the long stretch of a greenhouse across the far wall had green mould growing up inside the glass, and several of the roof panes were smashed. But all along the garden walls, there were apple and pear trees, set in between the twisted branches of giant fig, and the stalks of raspberry canes, blackcurrant and loganberries.

Wherever she looked, Seren could see the faded remains of the old kitchen garden. In the damp afternoon, it looked sad and forgotten. But Huw had been right. It was all there, just waiting to be brought back to life.

'It's beautiful,' she said, and there was no fooling anyone that she was about to let them walk away from this.

A gift of a job, Alun had called it, and, as far as Seren was concerned, that was putting it mildly.

3

Alun Caradoc looked up from his tray of seedlings and smiled across to where Seren was sitting, on the other side of the small conservatory where Caradoc Designs had started out, many years before. Seren was leaning over papers spread out on the stripped pine table, making notes and quick sketches in the book beside her.

'Alun,' she said.

'Yes, my dear?'

'Who is Chantrelle? Mother hasn't got a clue, and I've tried asking Matt, but he's hopeless. He just goes on about how wonderful she is, and how he's dying to meet her. Is she an actress?'

'Model,' Alun replied with a grin creasing the lines of his narrow face.

He was always faintly amused that Seren, who always had an unerring sense of what suited her slender figure, and best brought out the brilliance of her vivid blue eyes, had no more interest in the vagaries of fashion than her mother, who had always been eccentric when it came to clothes.

'Almost a — what do you call it?' Alun went on.

'Super model?'

'That's the one.'

'She's very beautiful,' Seren replied.

Of course, she thought, the photograph next to Huw's office really was from the pages of a glossy magazine. She frowned back down at the drawings in front of her.

'Problems?' Alun asked.

'No, not really. It's just hard trying to work out what someone you've never met will like. Some of these plants suggested just aren't practical here, and I've no idea what to suggest in their place.'

Chantrelle, it seemed, had about as much idea of gardening as Seren had of fashion. The proposed garden was to be filled with exotic blooms, clearly ones admired by the model during her travels. The delicate flowers of jasmine were to cover the walls, intermingled with honeysuckle, and several varieties of clematis and highly-scented roses, while, in the central beds, the exotic blooms of hibiscus and camellias were set amongst tropical palms and ferns.

As a romantic retreat, it would work well in the South of France, or on some tropical island. True, the castle was near enough the Gulf Stream to escape the harshest weather winter could throw at them, and many of the larger gardens nearby did contain magnificent specimens of the hardier kind of palm, but there was a limit.

'I'm not sure I can help you there, my dear,' Alun replied, delicately transferring seedlings. 'I can't say I've really met Chantrelle, except for the wedding, of course. She only contacted me because I've worked with Dylan before, and she knows he has always liked what I do.'

'Well, it is supposed to be a present for him. So, what kind of thing would he like?'

Alun brushed the soil from his fingers, and strolled over to the table. He looked down at the plans for a moment.

'Well, not a romantic, flower-filled bower, at any rate,' he said, at last, dryly. 'Not exactly a roses and honeysuckle man, as I remember.'

'Oh, dear.'

Seren looked at the plans with despair.

'It's supposed to be an anniversary present. It would be awful if it turned out he hated it. I'm sure his wife wouldn't be happy with that, either.'

Alun was looking more closely at Chantrelle's main sketch.

'It is a bit drastic. I don't know whom she had to advise her, but I'd certainly never have suggested taking out quite so much of the old planting.'

'That's what I feel.'

Seren pointed to the wall alongside

the greenhouse.

'Those old pear trees look really good trained along that wall. It would take years for anything to be able to replace them, as well as being a shame to destroy them.'

'I see what you mean. I expect she can see it all in her mind's eye as it will be, when everything has grown, and is just not thinking how bare it will look while the plants mature.'

There was silence for a while, while Alun went through Chantrelle's lists of plants.

'Mm,' he said, at last. 'When are you due back there?'

'Tomorrow morning,' Seren replied rather disconsolately.

'Right. I think we need to talk this over with Matt tonight. Then, if you both agree, I'll come with you and have a chat to Huw. He's a reasonable man. I'm sure he'll see the sense of what we are saying. Where did you say Chantrelle is at the moment?'

'South of France, I think.'

'Ah, well, I never thought I'd be saying thank goodness for e-mail, but at least we'll be able to show her our alternatives straight away. Time is short enough as it is, if you are to get this ready in time.'

'Thanks,' Seren said, more relieved than she liked to admit to herself. 'I know we are doing this on our own, but it is a special place, and it would be such a shame to spoil it.'

'Don't worry.'

Alun leaned over and patted her hand reassuringly.

'I'm sure we'll be able to come to some compromise on this.'

Alun was as good as his word. Matt and Seren arrived at the garden the next day, accompanied by Hefina, to find Alun already there, deep in facts, figures and reasoned arguments for the proposals they had worked out.

'Poor Huw,' Matt said, quietly. 'He doesn't stand a chance.'

Seren swallowed a giggle as the manager looked round, clearly relieved to see them all emerging from the doorway.

'Chantrelle was very specific,' he said, protesting, a faintly-harassed look on his features. 'It is meant to be a garden of love. I know she spent ages looking up the meanings of every plant.'

'It's a nice idea, don't get me wrong,' Alun replied. 'It's the practicalities that worry me. We could do exactly as she says on the plans. Trouble is, it would not look at all as she imagines, and one hard winter, and you could lose the lot. I think this is meant to be an expression of lasting love, isn't it?'

'Well, yes, of course.'

Huw scratched his head. He knew nothing about the practicalities of gardening, and Alun's reputation was second to none. If Alun Caradoc said there was a problem, then there was a problem. Matt and Seren had reached them, and he could see from a glance they were in agreement with their employer. In fact, Huw suddenly realised, it was most probably they who had raised the matter with Alun in the first place, looking for guidance from the older man's experience.

'What do you suggest?' Hefina asked.

She had been standing a little apart from the others, watching Alun's face intently.

'That we contact Chantrelle as soon as possible, and run a few alternative suggestions by her, and explain the situation to her,' he replied.

'Well, that seems reasonable.'

She turned to her brother.

'Don't you think, Huw? She can only refuse, in which case she'll only have herself to blame if things go wrong.'

Huw thought for a moment.

'OK,' he agreed, at last. 'You are welcome to use my office, if you like. They'll be out working on location by this time in the morning, but Chantrelle always checks her e-mails as soon as they break for lunch.'

'Fan mail,' Hefina put in, tartly, as if not quite able to help herself, but Huw ignored her.

'So we should get a reply this afternoon,' he added.

'Good.'

Having won his point, Alun was ready to take charge of operations.

'If Matt makes a start here, I'll write an outline of our suggestions, and Seren can draw Chantrelle some plans to show her what we mean.'

'Thanks,' Matt said. 'I always get the dirty work.'

He appeared quite cheerful about the fact, however, and the next moment this visibly increased.

'I'll help you, if you like,' Hefina was saying.

'You've never gardened in your life!' her brother exclaimed.

'Yes, I have,' she retorted, a faint colour rising to her cheeks. 'What do you know about it? You never visit my house unless you think there could be a chance of a free meal. You've never stepped inside my garden in your life.'

Huw appeared to be about to dispute

this, but something made him change his mind.

'OK, OK,' he said, watching her with a faint smile. 'I believe you.'

'There's so much to do here,' Hefina said, as if still continuing the argument, 'and it will get me out of the office for a while. It's always so hectic when Dylan or Chantrelle is here. It's really strange having them both away. I'm even running out of things to do.'

Huw, knowing how hard his sister worked on both Dylan's and Chantrelle's many business interests, somehow doubted this. But, as he had his own suspicions concerning her reasons for this unexpected offer, he kept his mouth shut.

'Fine by me,' Matt put in, before anyone else could disagree with the proposed arrangement.

'Good. I'll just go and change.'

Hefina vanished through the door.

'Enjoy your warm office,' Matt called, with a grin, as the others turned to follow her example.

'Enjoy the company,' Seren replied.

'And you.'

Alun, who was holding open the wooden door for Seren, looked at her closely as she passed, Matt's teasing comment in her ears. His eyes travelled back to Huw, just behind them, and a frown creased his brows.

'Hmm,' he muttered to himself, thoughtfully.

Hefina was back before Matt had finished fetching forks and spades and a strong-looking wheelbarrow from the van. She had changed from her business suit into a pair of scruffy trousers and an oversized jumper, complete with green wellies.

'I haven't any gardening gloves here, I'm afraid,' she said.

'No worries, we've plenty. I've brought you some. They're Seren's, so they should fit.'

'Thanks.'

He was rewarded with a grateful smile.

'So, where do we start?'

'Well,' Matt said and took a look

around the expanse of tangled garden. 'Since all the argument seems to be what happens along the walls, I think we should start in the middle and work our way out. I'm quite sure we won't manage to get there before they've finished persuading Chantrelle.'

'Great,' Hefina said, reaching for a fork.

'It's boring digging and weeding, I'm afraid.'

'Let me at it,' she replied.

They worked steadily for a while, digging over the first patch of ground, loosening the weeds. It was heavy work, which left them too breathless to exchange more than a few comments. But, as they slowed down, and Hefina began the process of removing the weeds and tossing them into the wheelbarrow, conversation started up again.

'Are you sure you don't mind about this?' Matt asked.

Hefina looked up from wrestling with a particularly determined dandelion.

'Quite sure. It's this, or staring at a computer screen, or keeping half-a-dozen prima donna businessmen at bay. No contest. Besides, I'm glad you and Seren questioned the plans. I'm not sure Dylan would like to see this garden prettified. And if he doesn't like something, there's all kinds of trouble.'

'I thought this was supposed to be a present. Surely his wife knows what he likes.'

Hefina hesitated, a faint look of embarrassment stealing across her face.

'Well, Chantrelle does tend to get these ideas into her head. Then she's impossible to argue with. I'm not sure how Dylan will feel about anyone messing with this garden. It was his mother's favourite place, you see. She tried to keep it as it had been, when it was a kitchen garden. She spent hours in here, weeding, tying up the beans and the peas, right up until she became ill. To be perfectly honest, I have a feeling he would rather keep this as it was.'

'Great.'

It seemed there was disaster ahead after all, Matt thought, a little nervously.

'Have you talked to Chantrelle about this?'

'Oh, I tried. I'm sure Huw said the same to her, but once she gets an idea into her head she doesn't give up, and, besides — '

She stopped abruptly, as if she had been about to let slip something she might regret later.

'Well, anyhow, if she's going to listen to anyone, it will be Alun. I'm not exactly the world's gardening expert.'

She stood up, rubbing her back.

'Tea?' she suggested, as if to change the subject. 'There's a flask in the greenhouse.'

Matt had no objections, and they made their way inside. The greenhouse seemed even larger once you went in than it did from the outside. Rows of old seed beds, made out of huge pieces of local slate, stretched along each wall.

The remains of a vine, badly in need of pruning, and with last year's grapes still rotting on the branches, twisted itself around the rafters almost the entire length of the building. Much of the rest of the space was taken up with broken pots, ancient bits of machinery, and half-used bags of compost that had seen better days. The air reeked of damp and peat.

'The electrician's coming tomorrow, so hopefully the heating will work, and there could be a kettle in here,' Hefina said, handing him a mug of steaming tea.

'Great.'

Mind you, he had no objections to things just the way they were, which seemed rather disloyal to Seren. He had been joking, when he teased her about the manager's admiring glances in her direction. For all his easy-going nature, Matt had never been one to believe in instant attraction. However, just at this moment, he was rapidly coming to the conclusion that he had been rather hasty about this, and it was likely to get him into trouble at any moment. He cleared his throat, and tried to keep his mind off the subject.

'Is anything else being done in here?' he asked.

''Fraid not. Chantrelle just said to tidy them up. To be honest, I don't think she knows what to do with a greenhouse.'

'Pity. With heating, there's amazing potential — grapes, oranges, lemons, pineapples. Bet the Victorians grew those.'

'I've never even seen tomatoes in here,' Hefina said. 'It seems awful. We all used to play here as kids, Huw, Dylan and I, and none of us has taken any interest since. Too busy with other things, I suppose.'

A wistful look had come over her face. Seeing her sitting there in the soft light from the glass panes of the greenhouse, streaked with dirt, the curls of her hair blown all over the place by the wind, Matt found himself over-whelmed by an impulse to just lean forward a little, and . . .

'Better get on,' he said gruffly, downing the rest of the tea in one gulp, and making his way outside. 'The others'll be back any moment.'

As far as Seren was concerned, it seemed the process of getting all the information to Chantrelle was going to take all day. Alun, thorough as ever, was not about to take any chances. She worked as fast as she could, sketching the detailed plans of the changes, along with an impression of how it would look straight away, and in a few years' time.

At the next desk, Huw was busy scanning in the photographs of shrubs and flowers Alun had brought with him, while Alun himself was typing away on the computer tucked into the seclusion of the far corner, frowning in concentration.

'Is that OK?' she asked at last, laying drawings on the desk beside him.

She was half expecting Alun to mutter for more detail as he had each time she had given them to him before, but this time he merely nodded.

'They'll do. Scan them in.'

'Why, you're really good, Seren,' Huw exclaimed in surprise, as he turned to look at the finished sketches.

'You tell her,' Alun muttered, looking up briefly from his screen. 'She should never have left art college.'

This was clearly an old argument. Huw raised his brows, but Seren merely smiled.

'I changed to study horticulture,' she said. 'I like to get my hands dirty.'

'Botanical illustrations, that's what you should be doing,' Alun said.

'One day, maybe. And what better way to learn about plants than to actually work with them? Alun is trying to persuade me to do the illustrations for his next book,' Seren explained in answer to Huw's quizzical look. 'I don't know why. There are plenty of others, with a lot more experience than me, who'd jump at the chance.'

'Coward.'

The remark came from the computer. Seren was used to this. She simply smiled, and let the subject drop.

'Ready,' Alun said.

All the evidence was there, waiting on its electronic journey halfway across Europe. Huw leaned over and began the electronic process. The three looked at each other — no turning back.

'So, do we do the deed?' Alun demanded, and the other two nodded.

'Here goes, then,' Huw said, taking the plunge, and turning to click on to send all the details to Chantrelle.

'And if that fails,' Alun said, 'there's always plan B.'

'Plan B?'

'The old-fashioned land-line.'

Alun nodded at the phone with a grin.

'And charm. It never fails.'

'Well, let's hope so,' Huw said.

4

'Meek as a lamb she was,' Huw said with relief, strolling down to the garden later that day.

Seren had already joined Matt and Hefina, and the three of them were loading the rubbish from the green-house into a skip.

'There are a few things she's set her heart on, but she's agreed to most of it.'

Matt was already looking happier. The prospect of disaster was receding again. He looked round the walled garden.

'She won't regret it.'

'Alun's just making out a new list of plants they agreed on. Chantrelle is back in two weeks, so she'll go through the rest of them with you then. And you can negotiate the bits she wants to keep. She might give in on some of them, but no chance on the rose and honeysuckle seat. She's set on that for the main photographs.'

'Photographs?'

Seren looked at him, puzzled.

'Oh, that's part of it. She'll have several glossy magazines lined up to photograph her and Dylan in the garden, in the summer, of course, when it's all in bloom.'

'That's always part of her little plans,' Hefina said drily. 'Magazines just love her.'

Across a mound of old netting they had been carrying between them, Seren met Matt's eyes.

'Magazines,' she mouthed.

Matt was looking suitably impressed. Huw seemed to have taken this aspect of the project for granted, and not seen it as worth mentioning. He could have no idea that for the two young gardeners this was huge. Their first garden was going to appear in a national magazine! Maybe more than one magazine, if they were lucky, and, given Chantrelle's obvious ability to attract publicity, it would not be some blurry snap tucked away in a corner. Never in a million years could they have hoped for such publicity, especially not so in taking over Caradoc Designs.

'So does Alun know about this?' Seren asked.

'Yes, of course,' Huw said, puzzled. 'That's why Chantrelle wanted the best. Surely he mentioned this to you?'

'Yes, of course,' Seren replied, hastily.

She glared at Matt, who seemed about to come clean and confess that Alun had done nothing of the sort.

'It slipped my mind, that's all.'

She tried to sound casual, as if their work had already featured in so many magazines one more could not possibly make any difference, but inside, tight knots were forming in her stomach. She looked across at Matt. They had to get this right. No room for slip-ups, or Alun's business would never be taken seriously again. And, if they got it right, well, they would have more publicity than they could ever have afforded, even in their wildest dreams. Get this right, and the world would be their oyster.

No wonder Alun had been so eager for them to take this job, and she could see why he hadn't mentioned just how public their efforts would be. At this stage it could have well and truly frightened them off. Now that the first shock was over, she could see the excitement beginning to sparkle in Matt's eyes, mirroring her own. Alun had been incredibly generous, giving them this chance. There could be no slip-ups, no disasters. They just had to make the most of it.

For the next few weeks, work in the garden went smoothly. Even the weather was on their side, spells of calm and sun punctuated by the odd day of blustery showers. The original garden had been laid out in large, rectangular patches, divided by narrow brick paths, just wide enough to manoeuvre the wheelbarrow.

Much to everyone's relief, Chantrelle

had followed the old layout, and set her swathes of colour between the paths. The only down side to this was that it meant that most of the digging and the weeding had to be done by hand, as there was no room to use a machine in most of the beds. At first, it had seemed an impossible task, but Alun, who was taking more than a passing interest in the progress of the work, suggested hiring an army of diggers.

'You won't get even half of it planted for this year otherwise,' he argued.

Huw could see the sense in this, and, as money was no object when it came to Chantrelle'schemes, he followed the advice straight away. The only person who was not happy was John, the broken-nosed guard on the gate, who could not contain his outrage as half the village, as he put it, came wandering into the grounds.

'I bet he's got a massive collection of cameras by now.'

Matt laughed as Huw was called away yet again to soothe the ruffled feathers of the indignant guard. But, however near it brought John to bursting a blood-vessel, Alun's tactic worked. A few days before Chantrelle was due back, Matt and Seren were able to look over the garden with satisfaction.

'I never thought we'd get this far,' Matt said.

'We only did it thanks to Alun,' Seren replied, thoughtfully.

All around them, the bare bones of the ancient kitchen garden had been revealed. Paths made their way between neatly-dug beds, leaving only the borders and the collection of damson and cherry trees at one end to be dealt with.

'Then the fun can begin,' Matt said.

The clearing away was satisfying, but he always preferred the creating that came afterwards. Seren could see he was just itching to get on to the planting, and the digging of a large pond near the middle of the garden. The pond was to have a fountain playing gently, illuminated at night by a myriad of hidden lights, and was planned to reflect Chantrelle's rose and honeysuckle arbour.

The arbour was to stand at the very centre of the garden, covering a large circular area of paving, large enough to hold a reasonable barbecue. The seat and the frame had been designed to run around the edge of the paved area, with an arch of wood above to support the roses and the honeysuckle that would eventually form a roof. The frame had already been commissioned from a local craftsman.

Alun had gone a few days before to inspect the half-finished piece, and returned muttering darkly about senti-mental clap-trap and vulgarity, but that was Alun, and there was nothing even he could do about it.

'Right, nothing for it, it's those pear trees next,' Matt said.

Seren sighed. Neither of them was looking forward to this, but it was getting late in the year to prune the fruit trees, and the pears had to be done.

'Come on then, might as well make a start. Let's get this over with. I hate digging up trees, however old.'

They struggled all morning, digging up the ancient roots, and burning the uprooted trees in a bonfire. It was dispiriting work, and by the middle of the afternoon, they had both had enough.

'Look,' Seren said, seeing the gloom in her friend's eyes as he eyed the next victim of his spade. 'There's no point in starting on a new one now. Why don't you go and check on those plants, and we'll finish this in the morning?'

'It'll mean a new bonfire,' Matt objected.

The suggestion was music to his ears, but he felt he had to be practical.

'We're going to need one soon, anyhow,' Seren said. 'Have you seen how many brambles there are in those borders? We're going to be burning stuff for at least a week.'

'Well, if you don't mind.'

Matt was caving in fast.

'Here I am, going to sit here doing nothing but watch a bonfire. D'you seriously think I mind?' she replied, and to that, there was no argument.

After Matt had gone, Seren sat for a while, feeding the orange glow at the centre of the fire. She had to admit that, after the hard work of the past few weeks, she was thankful for the rest. With the centre of the garden cleared, and Chantrelle due back the next day to sort out the final details of the plans, the urgency had gone. Really, she reflected, so much had happened in the past weeks, they seemed like a year. It was hard to take it all in.

Who would have thought it, as they made their way up the drive that fateful day, that they would be working on a garden destined to be seen all over the world? Certainly, she had never dreamed of meeting anyone like Huw. Seren smiled to herself. She was glad to see Matt and Hefina getting on so well, over these past weeks. There was a definite light to Hefina's smile whenever Matt was around, which, Seren mused, if her suspicions about Hefina's feelings for her employer were anywhere near the mark, was no bad thing.

From all that she had heard from the villagers who had been employed to help with the digging, Dylan Jones was not the easiest of men to work for, and Seren could only have sympathy for the assistant who had fallen for such a man, especially one whose wife was prepared to spend so much time and money on renovating an entire garden to demonstrate her love. Hefina must be finding all this work particularly painful, Seren thought to herself. She was glad that Matt seemed to be opening a way out from her predicament.

Mind you, if she was really honest with herself, part of her pleasure at seeing Matt and Hefina laughing easily together had more to do with the way it made Seren feel less guilty about her own feelings for Hew. Seren stirred the fire in front of her, and threw on the last of the branches stacked around her. What exactly did she feel for Huw? He certainly admired her. It hadn't taken Matt's gentle teasing to alert her to this fact, and he was certainly the most attractive man she had ever met.

The weeks had been so busy, she had been too tired to do much else at night except soak in a hot bath, and curl up in the luxurious warmth of her electric blanket, and Huw had known this. The rest of the diggers had made enough fuss about aching backs to cover everyone, but yesterday, as they stopped for lunch, Huw had turned to her as they made the tea in the greenhouse, out of earshot of the others.

'Maybe you would like to come for a drink one evening,' he'd said, sounding as if he was trying very hard to sound casual about it. 'When this bit is over, of course. There are some good pubs farther down the coast, with great views of the mountains.'

'I'd like that, thank you,' she had

replied, without needing even a moment to think about it.

'Good. I'll look forward to it.'

There had been no time for any further discussion, with the first kettle of tea ready, and thirsty diggers rapidly approaching the door. Seren had not told anyone, not even Matt, when he kept on asking her why she was grinning away to herself all afternoon. Somehow, she couldn't bear to be teased about Huw.

Seren was smiling to herself now. She shook herself, and rose to her feet. She looked at her watch. Matt was due back any moment. Meanwhile, she was growing stiff and cold with just sitting. She looked back at the fire. It was still glowing hot in the very centre. The wood around her had gone, but the trunk of the last pear tree they had been working on was almost up, just one last bit of root remaining. It would only take a few minutes' work. It took a long time and plenty of wood to get a fire this hot, and it seemed a pity to waste it, especially with such a large piece of timber to burn. It could be weeks before they had enough for such a big bonfire.

Mind made up, she walked back over to the garden wall, and took up her fork again. She was right, it was nearly out of the ground. She dug and pulled and twisted the stubborn last piece, until she felt the root give.

'Got you!' she exclaimed, triumphantly, as the old tree finally gave up the struggle, and she pulled it free from the surrounding earth.

'And just what d'you think you are doing?'

Seren swung round at the unexpected voice. Intent on her battle with the tree, she had not heard the garden door open, and the footsteps striding purposely towards her.

'Er — gardening,' she stammered out, her voice sounding feeble in her own ears.

'Destroying, more like. Have you any idea how long those pear trees have been there?'

The man before her was unmistakably furious. His dark eyes bore into her, almost taking her breath away with the intensity of his gaze. He was dressed in jeans and a dark leather jacket that had seen better days. Seren had only briefly glimpsed a photograph of the owner of Haulfryn Castle, in a newspaper cutting on Hefina's desk, but it was enough for her to recognise the new arrival as Dylan Jones himself, tall, dark, and fuming at the outrage to his property.

This was awful! He wasn't supposed to be in the country, let alone bursting in on his secret gift before it was even begun. Seren thought fast, trying to find a way out of this without giving the game away. Even the briefest reflection revealed there was nothing she could do, and, meanwhile, her silence seemed only to irritate him further.

'You can't just tear up trees like that,' he snapped.

'I'm not!' she returned indignantly.

'Oh, and this is your idea of pruning,

I suppose?' he demanded.

'Huw — ' she began.

The dark eyes under thick black brows glared at her with scorn.

'He'd better not be responsible for this,' Dylan said grimly. 'Right, I'm getting to the bottom of this. You stay here until I come back, and don't you dare lay a finger on anything else.'

The next moment, he had turned on his heel, and was striding rapidly through the gate.

For a moment, Seren could do nothing but obey him. She couldn't have moved, even if she tried. She fought down tears. After everything they had done, it seemed the whole thing was going to be a disaster after all, not that she wanted to plant anything for Dylan Jones at this moment, beyond an entire garden of deadly nightshade, she thought to herself, her temper beginning to rise. He'd stood there, shouting at her as if she was a schoolgirl, without even waiting for an explanation, and now he was rushing off to blame everything on Huw.

'Oh, no, you don't,' Seren said aloud, growing angrier by the minute.

Stopping only to throw a bucket of water over the fire, she ran after him towards the castle.

5

As she approached the manager's office, the sound of raised voices reached Seren's ears. Huw was trying to calm the situation, while the other was one Seren would be perfectly happy never to hear again.

'Don't!'

A hand stopped her from pushing the door open, and there was Hefina, slightly pale, standing behind her.

'But it's my fault,' Seren said. 'I was so surprised. I just couldn't think what to say, and now he thinks Huw is to blame.'

'Oh, Huw can take care of himself. He's used to it,' Hefina replied. 'And it's not your fault, Seren. Dylan came rushing back without letting anyone know. What else does he expect? I'm just sorry you got caught up in all of this. If he hadn't seen the smoke from the bonfire, he'd have come in here first, and Huw could have explained it all.'

'I just didn't know what to say, and I'm sure I've made things worse.'

'Oh, he'll calm down in a bit. He always does. Come on, I'll get you out of here.'

'What about Matt?'

'It's OK. I've already phoned him. Luckily he was delayed, and he hadn't left the nursery, so I said we'd meet him there. There's no point in you two getting caught up in all of this. Everything will be fine by tomorrow.'

'OK,' Seren said.

As she turned, the argument inside rose even further.

'Dammit, Huw, you should have known better,' Dylan was shouting.

'Come on, Dylan, you know what Chantrelle is like when she gets these ideas. What was I supposed to do? Forbid her to give you any anniversary present at all?'

'Don't be ridiculous. You might at least have warned me what she wanted to do.'

'Then it wouldn't have been a surprise, would it?' Huw returned, struggling with exasperation.

'Come on,' Hefina hissed, seeing her friend hesitate. 'Let's go.'

'And I wouldn't have come home to find some young girl massacring my pear trees.'

'Seren!'

But Hefina was too late. Muttering something along the line of, 'Right, that's it!' Seren had shot through the door, and into the room. Inside, the two men turned to frown at her.

'Speak of the devil,' Dylan muttered. 'I thought I told you to stay put.'

'I was not destroying any trees,' Seren said.

She looked very small and slight standing there in the doorway, and decidedly grubby, but there was a stubborn set to her mouth, and a glow to her cheeks. As far as Huw was concerned, she had never looked prettier.

'Oh? How do you work that one out?'

'Well, if you'd stopped to listen, I'd have told you.'

'I seem to remember I was not getting any answers.'

Seren met his scowl without blinking.

'It was supposed to be a secret from you, and you were supposed to be in New York, or wherever. How did you expect me to react when you turned up out of the blue like that?'

The dark eyes looked at her intently. Huw quickly hid a grin. No-one, not even Chantrelle, was in the habit of standing up to one of Dylan Jones's outbursts of temper, and his employer was looking slightly bemused at the unfamiliar experience.

'OK, I'm listening. Suppose you tell me now.'

'Thank you.'

'You're welcome.'

Huw only just managed to swallow a laugh at this exaggeratedly polite exchange.

'So?'

'We haven't taken out all of the trees,

only where they are too close together, and the dead ones.'

'So you burned the lot.'

'Of course not. Most of them are wrapped up in the greenhouse, ready for replanting. We are only burning the dead ones. They are full of fungus and disease, and they were infecting the rest. A few more years and you'd have lost all of them.'

The scrutiny of the dark eyes wavered just a fraction.

'And anyhow,' she pursued, making the most of her momentary advantage, 'I don't know what you are blaming Huw for. He was the one who helped persuade your wife not to get rid of the lot in the first place.'

There was a moment's silence. The next moment, Dylan removed his gaze from her face, and turned back to Huw.

'OK, let's start this one from the top, shall we?'

At least his tone was a little more reasonable. He seemed to have forgotten that Seren existed at all.

'Quick!'

Hefina shot round the door, and pulled Seren out with her.

'Just quit while you're ahead.'

To Seren's dismay, Hefina's face was wet.

'Hefina?'

'Oh, it's OK.'

On closer inspection, Hefina's eyes were sparkling, and Seren could see that she was struggling with laughter, rather than tears.

'What on earth is so funny?'

'You should have seen the look on his face. I wouldn't have missed that for the world. When you've been here longer, you'll see,' Hefina replied.

No chance of that, Seren thought to herself, as she followed her friend down the stairs, and out towards the waiting car. This time, I've well and truly blown it.

The next morning, the castle appeared deserted.

'Are you sure about this?' Seren said.

'Well, Hefina said to turn up as

usual,' Matt replied, looking around him dubiously.

'Well, I'm just collecting my tools and my gloves, and I'm out of here,' Seren replied.

'Maybe Hefina's right, and it has all blown over,' Matt said. 'After all, it wasn't your fault.'

'I'm not sure Dylan Jones sees it like that.'

'Look at it this way, at least his guard let us through.'

'Maybe he just wants the opportunity to yell at me again,' Seren replied gloomily.

She shouldered her rucksack, and began to make her way down to the walled garden.

'Oh, no,' she exclaimed suddenly. 'That's all we need!'

'What?'

'The fire. It's still smoking. I can't have put it out properly last night.'

Smoke was indeed rising steadily from inside the walls, quite a bit of it, not the wisp that might be expected from a dying fire. The two looked at each other. It looked as if the precious pear trees might have met an untimely end, after all.

As the two friends made their way through the door, the first thing they could see was the fire, not a raging fury destroying what was left of the garden, but a neat bonfire, exactly where they had left it yesterday, and next to it, carefully feeding small twigs into the growing blaze, was the bent head of a tall dark-haired man.

'That's him!' Seren hissed.

'Who?'

'Dylan Jones. Forget the fork and the gloves. I'm out of here.'

But already it was too late.

'Good morning,' the figure by the fire called, cheerful, friendly even.

''Morning,' Matt replied.

With a quick glance at his companion, he began to make his way towards Dylan. There was nothing for it. Seren followed, slowly.

'It's promising rain later,' he was

saying, as they drew near.

Yesterday seemed never to have happened. What was it that the rumours said about the family? Mad as hatters? Seren could quite see their point.

'So I thought I'd make a start. Get this going. After all, you don't want all this rotten wood hanging around for days, infecting everything.'

And that, Seren realised suddenly, was as near to an apology as she was likely to get. At least it meant he had accepted Huw's explanations, although it didn't mean she was any happier being within shouting distance of him. She was weighing up the pros and cons of making herself scarce, when Hefina appeared from the greenhouse. Whether she was there to ensure fair play or for reasons of her own, Seren was not quite certain. Either way, Hefina looked happy, which did not bode well at all for poor Matt.

'Looks good, doesn't it?' she said, looking around.

'Hm.'

Dylan had clearly used up his full quota of apologies for the day.

'We followed Chantrelle's plans closely,' Matt said anxiously, as if sensing this was not about to have a happy ending for them.

'Yes, I can see that. It was over-grown.'

Seren looked at him. There was something in his tone that was ominous. One look at the uncompromising set of his jaw, and the frown of those dark eyebrows and she was certain Matt's anxiety was justified.

'Look,' he continued, 'something did need to be done here, and I'm quite happy for you to carry on tidying. But I'm not having this place turned into some flowery set for Sleeping Beauty, whatever my wife thinks.'

From his tone, it seemed words had already been exchanged on the subject. Seren had the feeling that the happy couple were, at this moment, anything but happy, which would explain a decided absence of Chantrelle, even though she had been due to appear last night, and, unfortunately, the flush in Hefina's cheeks.

'It's such a pity,' Hefina was saying, 'especially after all this work. Surely something could be done with it, some kind of compromise.'

'No roses and honeysuckle in here,' he replied. 'And palms would just look out of place. I just don't see what, realistically, can be done with it.'

Seren looked around, with regret. She minded that she and Matt had lost their big chance to show Alun, and to give their running of Caradoc Designs a flying start, especially after Alun had given up so much of his time to help them. But, even more than that, she could not bear the thought of the place she had hoped to bring to life fall back into ruin and neglect, and that was what would undoubtedly happen if nothing was done with the place. Dylan was right, she thought, it was not a place to be prettified. Roses and honeysuckle would look out of place. There was nothing that could be done.

'Unless,' she said, suddenly, 'it was turned back into a kitchen garden.'

Lost in thought, she did not realise she had spoken aloud, until she suddenly became aware of the others staring at her.

'Restored.'

Matt caught her drift and she could hear the excitement in his voice.

'Now, that would be a project.'

Not that they were going to get the chance, going by the frown that met her across the fire. The suspicion was back in Dylan Jones's eyes.

'Are you always so good at talking yourself into a job?' he demanded.

'You don't have to use us,' she retorted, hackles rising once more. 'I'm sure you can afford anyone you liked, the best. I was saying what I thought. You can't let a place like this just die.'

'Really.'

His tone was irritated, and he appeared about to make the reply that would send them packing at that instant, but Hefina got there first.

'You're right,' she said. 'Come on, Dylan. Wasn't the National Trust always after this place? I'm sure they told your mother this was one of the finest examples of a Victorian kitchen garden in this part of Wales, in the whole of the UK, maybe. She'd have loved the idea, and it could still be Chantrelle's present to you, just modified. Then everyone will be happy.'

'It would be a big job. And you would have to know exactly what you were doing. There's no expertise like that around here. Even the National Trust admitted that.'

'But there might be plans.'

There was no mistaking the enthusiasm in Matt's voice.

'Plans?'

'Of the garden, as it was in Victorian times. There must be records.'

'You're right.'

It was Hefina's turn to catch the excitement.

'There are plans. I'm not sure how good they are, but they would be a start. They are in a box file, in the library. I can remember filing them there.'

Dylan looked at the eager faces around him. Given recent experience, Seren half expected him to fly off into a rage at this sudden hijacking of his plans. Instead, however, his face relaxed, and broke into a slow smile.

'Do I have a choice in this?' he demanded of Hefina.

'No,' she replied, laughing.

Without its customary frown, his was a handsome face, Seren suddenly realised. And, softened as it was at this moment by a smile, she could quite see how Hefina could fall for him, despite his sharp temper, and the fact that he was already married to one of the most beautiful women in the world. There was a certain charm in that smile that could get a girl into all kinds of difficulties if she let herself dwell on it too long.

'Are we on then?'

Matt was simply relieved that their employer appeared to regain his good humour, and that there was hope for them, after all.

'To look through the plans, see what's there? Well, if there's enough, we'll see,' Dylan replied.

'Fine,' Hefina said, quickly.

She knew from experience that they would get no more than that for now, and it was best to leave it while things were still so promising.

'Come on up for lunch, shall we say one-thirty?'

She looked towards Dylan, who nodded.

'One-thirty. I'll get the plans out. If the weather forecast is right, you won't be able to do much out here anyhow. And, Dylan, why don't you try and get hold of Alun, see if he can join us? If there's anyone who can tell if this is feasible or not, it will be him.'

'OK, I'll do that now.'

Seren smiled to herself at this sudden

vision of Hefina in her efficient personal assistant rôle. She was still reeling off a list of calls, apologies and appointments as they left.

'And I really think you ought to try speaking to Sian again,' she was saying, as they vanished through the door. 'She took all this very personally, you know.'

Alone in the garden, Matt and Seren looked at each other.

'A walled kitchen garden,' Matt breathed, still not quite daring to believe it. 'Restored to its original use. What a project. Can you imagine it?'

'Yes,' Seren said warily. 'But only if we are allowed to get that far, and Dylan Jones doesn't change his mind by the time he reaches the castle.'

'Oh, I'm sure Hefina will take care of that,' Matt replied, happily, entirely oblivious of the sharp look his companion threw in his direction.

6

'There you are, Alun,' Hefina said, placing a large box on the table. 'All the plans you could need.'

Alun Caradoc carefully brushed the last few crumbs away from in front of him, took hold of the box in his long fingers, and began to look through. The rest of them gathered round.

'Well?' Dylan demanded impatiently, after a few minutes. 'Anything?'

'I'm not sure. It's all extremely jumbled. Has anyone been through this?'

'Not to my knowledge,' Hefina replied. 'It all looked very tidy when I checked it before I put it on that shelf.'

'Well, it looks as if it has been shoved in any old how to me. Most of this is of no use at all,' Alan grunted.

Behind his chair, Matt and Seren exchanged disappointed glances. It seemed there was no hope after all. From the frown on Dylan's face, there appeared to be no chance at all of him changing his mind, should the plans not be found.

'There must be something,' Huw put in.

He was glad to see his employer's temper had quietened down, but this was rather dampened by the thought of the plans for the garden being abandoned, and no more mornings with Seren jumping out of the battered old van, and making her way through the wooden gate to start work.

'Enough to give a hint,' he added.

'I'm not hopeful,' Alun began, shaking his head. 'It looks like more of the same at the bottom.'

He paused, and began rifling through in earnest.

'Hello, now this is more like it.'

Eagerly, he lifted out a stack of papers. They were rather moth-eaten and yellowing, but the marks on them were still clear. Carefully, Alun unfolded them, one by one, and studied the drawings.

'These are the plans, all right. Very detailed, too.'

'And photographs.'

Hefina retrieved a collection of black and white prints that had fallen from between the papers. She picked up the print on the top and inspected it.

'So that's where Chantrelle got the idea of the rose bower,' she said thoughtfully.

She handed over the print to Dylan. Over his shoulder, Seren could just make out the sepia tones of a very old photograph. It must have been taken in midsummer. Heavy rows of peas and beans stood in front of the greenhouse, while, in the centre of the picture, a very pretty young woman, in the tight bodice and full skirts of Victorian times, sat on a seat, surrounded by an arch of roses.

'Let me see.'

Alun reached out, and surveyed the photograph for a moment, before handing it back to Dylan.

'There you are, you see,' he said, as if proving a point. 'Simplicity, elegance. You don't need fancy twirls and what-not.'

'Twirls?'

Dylan looked at him, distaste at the word visible on his face.

'Is that what I'm to be getting?'

'If whoever Chantrelle commissioned to make the seat follows her plans to the letter.'

Alun peered over his glasses.

'Or unless you get to him first. Nice idea, though,' he allowed. 'I like the way they've trained sweet peas amongst the roses. It must have made a relaxing place to sit. Looks as if there was some kind of similar covering over at least one of the main paths. Yes, very nice.'

'Do you know who it is in the photograph, Dylan?' Hefina asked. 'She must be related, she looks so like your mother.'

'I don't know. It would be my great-grandmother, I suppose. There must be a record somewhere. I'll have a look.'

'Whoever she was, she looks as if she loved the garden,' Seren said.

'Which is a reason for me to continue to employ you, I suppose,' Dylan returned, turning round with a frown.

'I didn't mean it like that!'

Why was it, whenever she opened her mouth, she seemed to offend this man?

'Well, whatever you decide,' Alun put in hastily, as if to prevent her from further embarrassment, 'the plans here and the photographs give sufficient information for someone to make a good stab at restoring the garden. I can recommend several firms who specialise in work such as this.'

Abandoning the plans, he took out his personal organiser from his jacket, and started to reel off a list of names. For a moment, Dylan frowned at him with irritation.

'Now Jacksons', they are a very well-established firm. Do plenty of work for the National Trust. I'd say they were your best bet. Give them a ring now, if you like.'

Alun pushed the organiser towards the young man. There was a moment's silence, and then, much to everyone's relief, Dylan Jones laughed.

'OK, OK, you win. You know I would far rather work with you, Alun, and you are the best. Even I realise that, you know very well!'

'Matt and Seren are Caradoc Designs now,' Alun pointed out.

'Fine. Then Caradoc Designs it is.'

He was looking down at the photograph again.

'It would be a pity not to finish the job.'

'And Chantrelle?' Alun was not giving up yet. 'I don't want Matt and Seren to find all this is to be stopped, or turned into some tropical paradise halfway through, you know.'

'I'll talk to Chantrelle.'

Dylan's smile was a little rueful.

'I'm sure she'll see that flower gardens are two a penny, but Victorian walled gardens are news. Besides, I'm sure there will still be plenty of roses around the seat for her photographs.'

'We'll make quite certain of that,' Alun replied.

★   ★   ★

She should, Seren told herself, be relieved that they still had work here, and that the plans for the kitchen garden were going ahead. Instead, over the next few weeks, she found herself growing increasingly uneasy.

'D'you think he's making sure we don't mess up?' Matt whispered, as the familiar figure made its way inside the garden.

'I don't know,' she answered.

'Not disturbing you, am I?' Dylan called as they turned to watch him settle down on the bench with the empty arch curving over it.

'No, not at all,' Matt replied cheerfully.

Dylan took out a sketch book, and

settled down to work. The two gardeners looked at each other, and then
continued with preparing rows for the
beans and vegetables, and pressing
ahead with the planting.

It seemed, Seren mused, laying down
seeds of carrots and onions in the patch
farthest from the arch, that he was
always there. His abrupt appearance
that first day had been taken for
granted by everyone else in the castle,
as if such unpredictable behaviour was
quite usual for him.

He had come back for a break, was
all Hefina told them, for a week. He
would be back in the States the
following Saturday. Since then, two
Saturdays had come and gone, and
there was still no sign of him leaving.
On the other hand, there was no sign of
Chantrelle at all. It seemed she had
agreed to the plans, but she showed no
inclination to rush home and supervise
the new garden.

'She's gone to their cottage in the
South of France,' Huw said. 'She likes

it there, and I expect she needs a break. Maybe Dylan is planning to join her, and leaving us to it.'

So far, however, Dylan was showing no sign of doing anything of the sort. Now and again he ventured out of the gates in the oldest, most beaten- up car Seren had ever seen outside of a scrap yard. This no doubt proved effective camouflage from the one or two reporters hovering hopefully at the gates following up rumours of something in the wind at Haulfryn Castle. Otherwise, he seemed to spend his time in the office with Huw, or sketching in the walled garden.

Despite her dislike of the photographer, Seren could sympathise with his wish to stay within the privacy of the barbed wire and the gates. She was tired already of running the gauntlet of reporters each time she and Matt arrived and left.

'Is it true? Are they really getting back together again, for good?'

This was the first question shoved

through the windows each morning, along with several flashing cameras, as if Dylan or Chantrelle might be hiding in the back along with the spades.

'Didn't know they'd split,' Matt would reply, good-humoured as ever.

'Come on, you know what they're like. On, off, on, off. You must have some idea.'

'Come off it. We're the gardeners. Can't you read, on the side of the van? Mr and Mrs Jones are hardly likely to discuss their private business with riffraff like us, are they?'

This was followed by a burst of laughter from the other reporters, allowing Matt to make his way down the road.

'Take no notice,' was Hefina's advice. 'I'll feed them a bit of publicity every now and then, and they'll soon realise Chantrelle really isn't here.'

Chantrelle, it seemed, was not in the habit of slipping out in ancient cars. The white Rolls Royce, brought out every now and then for cleaning, was more her style.

It was strange, Seren thought to herself, spacing tiny sage plants amongst the rosemary and oregano already establishing themselves in the herb garden. On the one hand, Dylan's constant presence made her as uneasy as Matt, waiting for the sudden flaring up of his notorious temper. On the other hand, these were also some of their most relaxed and happy times, particularly when Hefina joined them for coffee. It had continued to be a fine spring. Fresh sunshine lit up the garden, growing warmer each day, and with only the occasional patch of blustery rain. Most days, however busy she was, Hefina took time to sit with them in the garden, admiring their progress.

'We're very late for much of this stuff,' Matt said worriedly one day.

'It's worth trying, and there is always next year,' Dylan replied.

Some of the clam of the place

seemed to have rubbed off on him. Seren soon forgot to wait for his irritated yell, which never came.

'I do remember it looking like this, you know,' Hefina said one day. 'We were always being chased for eating stuff before it was ripe. I can still remember the stomach aches.'

'Don't remind me.' Dylan laughed.

'You sound troublesome,' Matt said, smiling.

'Oh, we were terrible.'

'It was Dylan and Huw led me astray, if I remember,' Hefina said.

'Of course. You hadn't learned to have fun until you met us.'

'Where did you meet?'

Matt was curious. The castle was so far away from the village, and it wasn't the kind of place you dropped into.

'Oh, at school. Even people in castles have to go to school, you know.'

'You make me sound like Little Lord Fauntleroy,' Dylan said.

He seemed to have forgotten his dignity and his bad temper, and was taking Hefina's teasing in perfect good humour. It was a great improvement, Seren concluded. There was no doubt Hefina brought out the best in him. Poor Hefina. She was probably aware of the fact, too, Seren thought, sadly.

'Not a bit of it. You could be a right spoiled brat, at times.'

'Rubbish! I know I've got a bit of a temper.'

'A bit!'

'All right. I lose my temper easily.'

'You can say that again.'

'You make me sound totally unreasonable,' he protested.

'I rest my case,' she replied.

'Well, then, you should have stayed with your hot-shot businessmen in London,' he retorted.

For a moment, Hefina did not reply. The laughter had gone, and she went first red, and then very white. Dylan was looking sorry, as if he knew he had said something bound to hurt her.

'Although,' he added more gently, 'I don't know any other assistant who would put up with my unreasonably vile temper for so long.'

Hefina smiled, and the moment was over, although the light-hearted banter was not resumed.

'I didn't know Hefina worked in London,' Seren said, after her friend had returned to the office. 'I thought she had always worked here, like Huw.'

'Oh, no,' Dylan replied. 'She's a real high-flyer is Hefina. She worked for several of the largest firms in the City. She's only been back here eighteen months or so.'

Something told Seren not to ask the reason why Hefina had returned. Maybe there was some truth in the reporters' questioning. Perhaps the Jones' marriage had been on the rocks, after all. Although not now, it seemed, going by the attention that they were currently being paid to lavish on this garden as a wedding anniversary present.

Matt said nothing, just returned to working at the other end of the garden, as if he wished to keep his thoughts to himself, although it was strange, Seren was to think, more than once over the next few weeks, as they drank their coffee in the sunshine, that Chantrelle was never mentioned by Dylan or Hefina. It seemed almost as if her presence was irrelevant to the castle, as if she was never coming back, or had never existed.

She was musing over these thoughts, late one afternoon, when she found Dylan standing near her, watching her tie the first shoots of peas to the wigwam of canes that was to support them. He had his sketchbook closed in one hand, and was looking thoughtful.

'Not too much slug damage,' she said.

His silent presence made her slightly nervous, and she was glad to try and strike up a conversation, to distract her mind from the delicate task at hand.

'The gravel and egg-shells seem to be helping. I'm glad we decided to go as organic as possible, and do without the slug pellets.'

'So am I.'

From the tone of his voice, however, his mind seemed elsewhere.

'Huw showed me your sketches,' he resumed abruptly, after a moment's silence. 'They're very good. You've quite a talent there.'

'Thank you.'

The warmth of this unexpected praise spread slowly through her. She was quite certain he was not a man to say a thing like that unless he meant it. However, her pleasure was slightly marred by a feeling this was leading up to something. To what, she was not entirely sure. She smiled at him.

'Huw said you may go back to it at sometime.'

'Maybe. We'll see.'

She wished he would just go away. Was that what he wanted to talk about, painting? She was curious to see what he had been working on in that book of his, but the idea of such a personal conversation made her uneasier than ever. She was beginning to understand how Hefina could have remained captivated by such a contradictory man, at one moment totally unreasonable, the next turning with a slow smile that could set pulses racing. She was rapidly coming to the conclusion that Dylan Jones was best kept as far away from as possible.

'It's nearly time to go.'

She sounded feeble, even to herself.

'I must help Matt pack things away.'

'Of course.'

He half turned away, as if to go. The moment she thought she was safe, he was back again.

'The thing is . . . ' He hesitated, looking at her intently with those dark eyes. 'The thing is, I've an invitation to the preview of a painting exhibition.'

Seren looked at him, blankly.

'I'm not usually much of a one for such things, but the artist is one of the best, and it would be a good place to meet people. I could introduce you.'

'You're asking me to go with you?'

'Yes. It's tomorrow evening, about nine. I can pick you up, or you can stay and have a meal here.'

'No. That's very kind of you, but I can't.'

Her reply was rather more abrupt than she had intended it to be.

'I see.'

He nodded pleasantly, but he couldn't quite hide his disappointment at the rebuff.

'I'd like to. That is, it was thoughtful of you to ask.'

Seren was conscious of digging herself in deeper by the minute. She wasn't going to tell him exactly why she couldn't go with him. She would die of embarrassment.

'It's just I'm already going out.'

It sounded like a clumsy lie. She took a deep breath, and collected her thoughts together.

'It's my mother's birthday tomorrow. We're taking her out for a meal in the evening. The table has been booked for weeks.'

He still looked unconvinced that she wasn't just making up a story to get out of the invitation. But he could hardly accuse her of lying to her face. Instead, he smiled politely.

'Enjoying your evening then,' was all he said.

'Thanks, maybe another time,' she added, in spite of herself, but he was already walking away.

There wouldn't be another time, which should be a relief, but it wasn't.

7

In Haulfryn village art gallery, the preview party was in full swing. Earlier in the evening, the room had been so full it had been difficult to move, let alone take a closer inspection of the large, brightly-coloured canvasses adorning every wall, or even speak to the artist herself. It was now growing late, and many of the guests had started to leave.

Any exhibition by Rhianna Richards was eagerly awaited, attracting admirers from the surrounding valleys and far beyond. You were never quite sure whom you might meet.

Rhianna was making her way around the room, enjoying herself immensely. She was a slight figure, dressed in a long skirt of purple silk. Never one to be shy about her age, it stated clearly on each morsel of publicity that she was exactly fifty-six. Even with very little make-up, however, her skin still had a youthful glow, while her dark hair was streaked with very little white. Her beauty might have faded a little with time, but it had always been her eyes that had been her best asset, and those were still the same, warm and sparkling, and with a scarcely suppressed mischief lurking just beneath the surface.

'Well, I never.'

One of the younger men next to her paused in his deep discussion of light and shade, and turned to stare at the door.

'Look who's here, and I thought she was supposed to be in France for at least the next month.'

Rhianna followed his gaze, to where a tall, slender woman in a figure-hugging gown of pale blue was stepping gracefully through the door. She paused, framed in the doorway, adjusting the long, fine ringlets that fell around her, right down to her waist, while her deep blue eyes surveyed the scene. She had the kind of beauty that had heads turning throughout the room, as she turned to slip her arm through that of her companion.

'Oh, no, and she's brought that husband of hers with her,' the young man's neighbour remarked. 'I thought she'd got rid of him ages ago.'

'Apparently not.'

Rhianna had been scrutinising the young woman closely, but now an amused smile was playing around her lips.

'Husbands do have their uses, you know.'

But neither young man was listening, both of them being too busy making their excuses, and hurrying to where Chantrelle was already surrounded by a flock of admirers. Far from being offended at this desertion, Rhianna laughed, and beckoned to the dark-haired man making a rapid escape from the scrum.

'Dylan!' she called. 'Over here.'

Dylan, who had been frowning at the edge of the room, contemplating a rapid exit as soon as he reasonably could, joined her with some relief.

'Hello, Rhianna,' he said, kissing the older woman on the cheek. 'These paintings look beautiful, what I can see of them.'

'It's been a long time,' she replied, with a slight reproach in her voice.

'I know, I know. I've been busy, too much going on.'

'So I hear,' Rhianna replied drily. 'Well, I'm glad you came tonight. I know how you hate these things.'

'To be perfectly honest, I didn't really intend to. I was going to come and see your work during the week, when it is quiet, but then Chantrelle arrived back this evening, and you can't keep her away from something like this.'

'So I see.'

Rhianna smiled, highly entertained at the sight of the crowd gathered around the famous model.

'Still, I'm glad you came. I want to

have a word with you.'

'Oh? What about?'

'Painting.'

Dylan frowned at her, but before he could question her further, her attention was already being called away by others among her guests.

'I'm going soon,' she said rapidly. 'So, if I don't have a chance to speak to you again, make sure and give me a ring.'

'As you wish,' he replied, quite obviously intrigued.

The next moment, she had been enveloped by the crowd. Dylan returned to his place next to the wall, and inspected the nearest painting. He had always disliked crowds, particularly when all he wanted to do was concentrate. He looked around with rising irritation. How on earth did he get himself talked into this in the first place? He was just about to make his way over to Chantrelle, to tell her that he was leaving, when a movement in the doorway caught his attention.

Trust Alun to be late, he thought, amusement breaking through his irritation as he recognised the tall, white-haired owner of Caradoc Designs. And trust him not to be alone. Dylan was frowning again. He had only ever met Rhianna briefly, but he liked and admired the artist, and had no wish to see her feelings hurt. It was no secret that, since the death of her husband some five years before, Alun had been dancing close attention, as if determined not to lose her again. As if those old rumours of why he had never married had been true. He even appeared to have given up the lifetime habit of constantly having a beautiful young woman on his arm, until tonight. At this moment, he had bent down to speak quietly to the elegant young woman in a simple dress of green cotton. Dylan frowned at the companion, who had turned to smile at the older man with obvious affection. The next moment, his frown deepened to a positive scowl.

'Dylan! I didn't think you'd be here.'

Alun had spotted him, and was making his way over.

'There you are, Seren, I told you it must be Chantrelle over there. There is no-one like her.'

'No-one,' Dylan replied.

He looked pointedly at Seren, whose cheeks had gone bright red, and who could not quite meet his eye. Alun was oblivious.

'We'd have come earlier, if we'd have known, wouldn't we, Seren? These can be deadly affairs at times, you know.'

'Yes,' Dylan replied coolly.

But, for all his quick temper, he was not one to bear a grudge, and though Seren was not at this moment his favourite person in the world, he had no wish to deepen her obvious embarrassment.

'I didn't know I was coming myself,' he explained. 'Chantrelle came back this evening without telling anyone or I wouldn't have bothered.'

Seren shot him a grateful glance.

What on earth must he be thinking of her? If only she'd just come clean about this evening in the first place, instead of making such obviously feeble excuses that just had him thinking the worst.

'Alun!'

It was Chantrelle who saved them from further awkward moments, sailing towards them, admirers in tow.

'As beautiful as ever,' Alun said, gallantly, kissing her hand.

Chantrelle was delighted.

'Now, just why did that habit die out, do you suppose?' She laughed, looking around her. 'You always did know how to treat a lady, Alun. You can kiss my hand any time.'

Amusement rippled out around her. Chantrelle, Seren could see, was someone who would always attract attention, just as if she were standing on a stage, and all those around her were her audience. If possible, she was even more beautiful in reality than in the photograph. Her skin was flawless, and her blue eyes deep and piercing. There was a delicacy about her, a fragility that would make any man want to sweep her up and protect her, she thought, with an inward sigh. Wrapped in her own thoughts, she had hardly noticed Dylan breaking through the hilarity to introduce her.

'And this is Seren, Chantrelle, who is helping to make such fine work of your garden.'

'Really?'

Chantrelle's eyes flickered briefly over the young woman in the plain dress, no heels, with her hair hanging loose, and not a scrap of make-up to be seen, and clearly found her of no further interest.

'Anyhow, it's not my garden, my dear. It's yours.'

Even Dylan, who was used to Chantrelle's rebuffs of people she thought beneath her, was speechless for a moment. By the time he had recovered himself, his wife was moving away, clinging determinedly to Alun's arm.

'Have you seen who's over there, Alun?' she was saying.

'Who might that be?'

'Alex Rylance, the film director. Don't you just love his movies?'

Dylan and Seren watched the two walk away. This time it was his turn to be embarrassed.

'I'm so sorry. I don't know what got into her. That was inexcusable.'

'That's OK.'

Seren smiled at him. To his surprise, she appeared amused rather than offended, and her own embarrassment was fading.

'After all, there is only one Alex Rylance, even if he does have more hands than an octopus.'

Dylan looked at her sharply. For a moment, she made it sound as if she met famous directors every day of her life, which would be just Alun's style and a clear sign that this was not the first time they had been out together.

'Look, I'm sorry about the other day,'

she was saying. 'I should have explained better.'

'That's all right.'

His sense of dignity was back, and he spoke abruptly.

'I shouldn't have put you on the spot like that. What you do in your own time is really none of my business.'

'But I want to explain.'

'There's no need.'

They stood in mutual distrust for a while. Any attempt at conversation was clearly going to get them nowhere, Seren thought sadly. They seemed doomed to talk at cross purposes. Dylan, meanwhile, was attempting to resurface his manners.

'Would you like to go round and see the paintings?' he offered in cool politeness.

'It's all right. I've seen them.'

'You've only just got here!' he exclaimed.

'So? And what makes you so sure I haven't been able to see them before?'

'Rhianna has always been paranoid

about showing her work before it is previewed.'

'Don't believe all you read in the papers,' she replied.

'And what was there about me in the papers?'

It was Rhianna, who had quietly joined them, and was watching the pair with amusement.

'Nothing,' Seren said.

'Nothing at all,' Dylan almost echoed her.

'Well, I'm glad to hear it. I have to go now, Dylan. Sorry I didn't have time to speak to you properly. Just don't forget to call me.'

'I'll get your coat,' Seren muttered, anxious to get out.

'Nonsense. Alun can do that.'

Rhianna looked over to where Alun had not even removed his arm from Chantrelle's.

'It will also remind him he is supposed to be on his best behaviour,' she added dryly. 'You continue your conversation, Dylan. I can't wait to see this garden, you know. Photographs don't really give you a proper idea of something like that.'

'No.'

Dylan was distracted. There was something here that didn't quite add up. Rhianna Richards, known for her unfailing courtesy to all those she met, and her kindness towards all young artists, was behaving as if she barely noticed Seren's existence, while Seren herself had the appearance of becoming increasingly uncomfortable, as if she had more than a passing thought to banish abruptly. Rhianna caught the crease forming between his brows, and mischief began to dance within her beautiful eyes.

'I bet you didn't know you were one of Seren's heroes,' she remarked all of a sudden.

'No, he's not!'

Seren flashed the denial back hotly, aware of the colour rising in her cheeks.

'You are, you know. When she was little, she used to spend hours gazing at those seascapes of yours, the ones I bought from that first exhibition of yours, and told you to stick to the painting, and make them priceless one day, remember? But you betrayed my faith in you, and went off chasing models instead.'

Dylan's frown had become decidedly black at this mild chiding, but Rhianna ignored it.

'Well, anyhow, Seren certainly loved them. She spent hours copying them. Started her drawing, in fact. Far more than my efforts ever did.'

She met Dylan's bemused look, and chuckled wickedly.

'And I suppose Seren just forgot to mention that she is my daughter.'

Rhianna laughed out loud.

'Now, that is Seren all over. Never acknowledges me in public, you know,' she added, with mock distress. 'Do you, darling?'

'Mam!'

'Well, it's true.'

'Only because you always manage to

embarrass me,' Seren returned, faintly exasperated.

'Nonsense.'

Rhianna kissed her daughter affectionately, still enjoying the sight of Dylan attempting to adjust to this unexpected turn of events.

'And it's your birthday today,' he managed at last.

'So it is. Number fifty-five, but don't tell anyone. Always admit to being older than you are. It always impresses people with how good you look for your age. And don't shake your head like that, Seren. Just you wait, it'll come to you one of these days.'

'Yes, Mam,' Seren replied.

When her mother was in this mood, there was no telling what she might say next, and she had no desire to encourage her.

'Anyhow, Dylan, we must love you and leave you. Just don't forget, I've still got a bone to pick with you about your painting. The next exhibition I want to see here is yours. I've got to protect my investments, you know.'

Somehow, there was a charm about the artist that made it quite impossible to be offended by her pronouncements. Despite himself, Dylan found he was responding to the twinkle in her eyes.

'Enjoy your evening,' he replied, with his slow smile.

'Oh, we will. I'd ask you to join us, but the table's booked, and knowing Alun it will be the kind of place you have to put your name down at birth.'

'No, it isn't,' Seren said. 'I made sure he chose a place where you can relax, though I expect it will be full,' she added hastily, glancing at Dylan who was now watching her thoughtfully.

'Well, it's time we left. I shall just have to drag him away.'

'I was telling you the truth,' Seren said, as Rhianna made her way towards the distant group.

'So I gather,' he replied, looking at her with undisguised curiosity. 'You just forgot to mention that the artist I was trying to take you to see was such a close relative.'

'You didn't ask.'

'No, but it's not exactly the kind of question you put, out of the blue, like that, and the information just might have explained things.'

'True. Sorry about that. I didn't want to be rude. I just hate all this, and I hate having to explain about it all the time.'

'And that is the reason Alun brought you here?'

'Why else? You didn't think I was one of Alun's girls, did you?'

'Well, what else was I supposed to think?'

'Thank you very much. Didn't you know he's turning over a new leaf?'

'A new leaf?'

'Leaving all the girlfriends behind, proving he can be a respectable married man.'

'And if not?'

At the other side of the room, a rather reluctant Alun was being prised away from Chantrelle, and sent in search of Rhianna's coat.

'Well, in that case, Mam's told him he doesn't stand a chance with her, however many times he begs her to marry him. That's a secret, even if not a very well kept one. Please, don't tell anyone I said that.'

'Of course not.'

Dylan found his good humour returning.

'Don't tell me we are witnessing the taming of Alun Caradoc.'

'I'm afraid so,' Seren replied with a laugh.

8

'And how did the birthday party go?' Dylan Jones asked as he sauntered through the gate into the walled garden.

'Oh, fine, thanks.'

Seren looked up with a smile. He waved to Matt who was busy tying up fruit canes on the opposite side, pulled out one of the more serviceable garden chairs from the greenhouse, and settled down with his sketch pad.

'It's looking good,' he remarked as he looked around.

'Isn't it?' Seren replied, with satisfaction.

The bare earth was now dotted with neat patches of green shoots, while fresh tendrils had begun to make their way up the carefully-positioned wigwams of cane. Not so long ago it had still seemed an impossible task but, suddenly, it all seemed to have come together. She could hardly believe that this week was to be their last.

They would be back, of course. A place like this would need regular maintenance but it would not be the same as being here five days a week, almost from dawn to dusk. It had not struck her before just how much she could miss it. The bringing back to life of the garden had occupied her every waking thought for the past few months.

But there was nothing for it. They had plenty of other work which could wait no longer. Alun had taken over their regular bookings, supervising a couple of the seasonal workers he usually took on in the summer when things got really hectic. But now there was no need. It was time to move on.

Seren sighed to herself and returned to fastening up the shoots of the sweet peas to the frame of the seat.

'A penny for them.'

Dylan was busy sketching but nothing escaped him.

'Oh, nothing. It's always a bit sad when you come to the end of something like this. And no, I am not angling for a full-time job,' she replied to his quizzical gaze. 'It's the same with any big project, and you did ask.'

She was expecting the frown to make an appearance but, instead, he laughed, causing Matt to look up from tying beans at the unexpected sound.

'That's very defensive.'

'Only because you keep on accusing me of things,' she retorted.

His unusual good humour remained unruffled.

'You're just imagining it,' he replied.

Seren was about to respond to this, when something in his look stopped her.

'Are you trying to wind me up?' she demanded.

'Would I do a thing like that?'

'In a word, yes.'

He laughed again, causing Matt, who was stretching to reach a distant shoot, to almost fall over.

'Aren't you afraid of anything, Miss Evans?'

Seren looked at him, puzzled at this unexpected comment.

'Of course I am. Broken-nose scares me witless.'

'Broken-nose?'

'John, on the gate.'

'Oh, John. John is meant to scare everyone witless. He was hired specifically for his ability to terrorise tabloid hacks into oblivion. And you can't get more scary than that.'

Clearly nothing was about to disturb this uncharacteristic good humour.

'Broken-nose suits him, by the way.'

'Please don't tell him. We've still got to go past him twice a day for the next week. I'd never be able to look him in the eye again.'

'I wouldn't dream of it.'

His tone was serious, although there was a glint in his eyes she didn't quite trust.

'No,' he said, resuming the former conversation, 'I meant closer to home.'

'You've lost me.'

'Me.'

'You? Why on earth should I be scared of you?'

'Well, I've managed to spend half the time roaring at you and making it obvious I've come to the worst possible conclusion about you. And, besides, that unfortunate temper of mine has a certain reputation. According to the tabloids, half the models have refused to work with me.'

'I don't read tabloids,' she replied.

'No, of course you don't. Neither do I, any more. Otherwise, I might have remembered that Rhianna's married name was Evans, and put two and two together. Even I can come up with the answer to that one.'

'Sorry about that.'

'Don't apologise. It serves me right for being so patronising.'

'You weren't patronising! It was kind of you. And you were right, what you said last night. I should have explained. It was just so, well, unexpected. It threw me.'

'That's OK.'

'No, it isn't.'

She looked at him earnestly. This was probably her one chance to clear the air between them and, even though she would probably never see him again, she wanted above anything that they parted on good terms.

'I've spent all my life trying to get away from all that, from being Rhianna Richards' daughter. When I was a kid, she was always so beautiful and so outrageous. There were always photographers and reporters. We could have done with a castle, and a John on the gate,' she added ruefully.

'Which is why you use your father's name.'

'Yes.'

'And left art school?'

'I suppose so. I wanted to make my own way, do my own thing. Whatever I did, I was always compared to her. I don't want that. Doing the gardening, even though it was Alun who gave me a job, and is practising keeping a fatherly eye on me, it's something different.'

'But you'd still like to get back to the drawing.'

He had put down his pencil and was scrutinising her closely.

'Yes, I suppose so. It's why Alun wanting me to provide illustrations for his book is so tempting. It's the kind of thing I like best, but I just don't want to be caught up in doing something because he wants to please Mam.'

She found Dylan still watching her, a serious expression on his face.

'Well, can you bear an outsider's advice, no shouting, no patronising?'

'Yes, please, it's just what I need.'

'Well, I would say that Alun may well be influenced by you being your mother's daughter, but he is also a professional, and a perfectionist. And, I would say he wouldn't dream of having anything associated with him that wasn't of the best, whatever his personal involvement.'

'I never thought of it that way. You're

right. Of course he wouldn't.'

'If I was you, I'd take the chance. You might not get another for a long time. Always stick out for what you love best.'

A touch of the old bitterness had crept into his face.

'Don't you?'

'You're right. I'm good at giving sound advice, just not at taking it.'

'I didn't mean that.'

They had strayed into dangerous territory and Seren was not altogether clear what it was exactly they were now talking about. It looked as if they were to end on a misunderstanding after all. All of a sudden, Dylan pulled himself back out of his bad humour.

'Yes, I know, and you're right. I should have listened to your mother in the first place and stuck to painting. I was too impatient for success. I know now that I should have trusted that the few that sold would grow, and that your mother's instinct was right. Instead, I went for overnight success, fame and fortune, and Broken-nose threatening all my visitors. The irony is, I could now sell all my old paintings ten times over.'

'So why don't you? Start again, I mean.'

'I'm a fashion photographer, not some painter in a garret.'

'Then you are right. You are not very good at taking your own advice.'

'Hmm,' he grunted, and the next moment he was striding out of the garden.

'What on earth was all that about?' Matt enquired.

'I'm not sure,' Seren said.

'They're right in the village. Moody devil, isn't he? Well, at least you made him laugh, I suppose.'

'And storm out in a temper.'

'Don't worry. We'll be out of here soon. I don't know how anyone manages to put up with him.'

'No,' Seren said quietly.

As the end of their last week approached, Seren found she could hardly wait for Friday to arrive. With both Dylan and Chantrelle in the castle, the entire atmosphere had changed. There was a tension in the air which you could cut with a knife. Seren missed their cheerful coffee breaks with Hefina. Dylan was hardly ever there, slipping out each morning in his car on some business or other. Hefina scarcely made it out of her office, and only then for a harassed flight from one end of the corridors to the other.

'I am not her secretary!' Seren heard her exasperated exclamation, as she went up for coffee with Huw one day.

'I'll have a word, if you like,' Huw said sympathetically.

'And have her thinking I've been telling tales? No, thank you. I'll deal with this my way.'

She shot out of the office, nearly flattening Seren with a huge sheaf of papers.

'Sorry!' she called. 'Don't mind me. I'm just off to commit murder.'

'Is this a bad time?'

Seren looked at Huw who had the air

of someone nearing the end of their patience.

'No, it's fine. Take no notice. It always gets like this when they are both here.'

'Right.'

Being Huw, he was being too diplomatic to add that Chantrelle was not exactly Hefina's favourite human being. Did he also suspect the reason why, she wondered.

'It does seem to have become quite lively. I hope it's not the garden again.'

She was prying, she admitted it to herself. Part of her was disgusted at such subterfuge. The rest of her was hanging on his every word.

'Not your part of it. They are both more than happy with that. It's the arrangements for the photographers. It always ends up like this. Forget it. Nothing for you to worry about, and it always gets sorted out in the end.'

'Good.'

His smile was particularly attractive, she noticed, with the first stirrings of regret at leaving tomorrow. Somehow, since Dylan had arrived, she and Huw seemed to have grown apart. He had had much more to do, of course, but she was also aware that her attention had been distracted, taken elsewhere. She had not realised before just how much space in her thoughts had been taken up by the owner of Haulfryn.

She looked again at Huw. What on earth had she been thinking of? There she had been pitying Hefina for falling into a trap with no happy ending possible, and she had been in danger of falling into the very same trap herself, without even realising it. And, more to the point, she had been too preoccupied to take the chance to get to know this generous and attractive man before her. By tomorrow, it would all be too late.

'Huw,' she began, but before she could continue, there was a smart rap of heels on the corridor outside, and the door was pushed open.

'Huw, can you just — oh.'

Chantrelle paused, took in the other occupant of the office, briefly, and chose to ignore her.

'Can you just find the name of the photographers we used last time? Hefina seems to have vanished.'

There was no doubt about it, even in the light of day, and in her everyday clothes, Chantrelle's beauty was breath-taking. The fine tendrils of her hair were swept up carelessly into a blue velvet ribbon, leaving just a few to fall either side of her delicate face. Her top clung to her slender figure, and her jeans were cut in the latest fashion.

I could never look like that, however hard I tried, Seren thought ruefully.

She caught sight of the immaculately-shaped and polished nails, and hid her own scratched and grubby hands quickly. No wonder Chantrelle had the effect of making Huw look at her in the same star-struck manner as Matt still mentioned her name.

'Hefina is very busy,' Huw said gently. 'And she is still trying to find a flight for Dylan.'

'But I told her not to bother. He needs to be there for the photograph. It's his present. I need him. He has plenty of time to get back to the States before the shoot starts again.'

'I'm sorry, Chantrelle, but Hefina does take her orders from Dylan. And he is quite determined on taking the first flight he can get.'

'I don't see why. This is his home.'

There was a spoiled pout to her lips, Seren noted, taking a quick glance at Chantrelle. She had the look of someone used to getting her own way, and was quite prepared to throw a childish tantrum to get it. Maybe there was more than simple jealousy in Hefina's dislike of Dylan's wife.

The thought opened up other avenues. Having avoided any tabloid gossip and local rumour for as long as she could remember, Seren had recently found herself risking being confronted with some idle piece of tittle-tattle about the renewed romance between her mother and Alun, to have a quick skim through the most likely offenders. Apart from a glowing write-up on the exhibition, there was no mention of Rhianna Richards. Of Dylan and Chantrelle, on the other hand, there was plenty, and most of it on the subject of how they were never seen in each other's company these days.

'Let me know when Dylan is back, Huw. I'll speak to him.'

And what if the rumours were true? They could have nothing to do with her. If Dylan and Chantrelle were finally heading for a separation, then it would be Hefina who should be happy, not her. Seren remembered those carefree coffee breaks in the garden, and just how improved Dylan appeared when he was in Hefina's company.

'Poor Matt,' she sighed to herself.

Matt had never let anything slip about how things stood between himself and Hefina. For once, he seemed oblivious to all the undertones at the castle. He had been the one to give a wry laugh when they left late in the evening to find two lights on in the castle, each at opposite ends of the building.

'A real sign of conjugal bliss,' he had remarked, as if what he was supposing had no implications for him whatsoever.

'Chantrelle . . . '

She came back to the present to find the model had gone, and Huw was rising to follow her.

'I'm sorry, Seren. Can we do this another time? I need to sort this out before Dylan comes home.'

'No problem,' Seren replied, forcing her voice into light-hearted tones.

9

'Last day,' Seren said, finding it hard to hide her relief as she smiled as sweetly as possible at Broken-nose, who gave her a grudging nod of recognition.

'So, they are getting back together then?'

The usual reporters' heads were thrust in at the windows as the van slowed to a halt.

'It is true they're renewing their vows for their anniversary?'

'In the garden you've been working on?'

'They could be planning to have a Roman orgy in there, for all we know.'

Matt was getting used to this line of questioning, and his sense of humour was always threatening to get the better of him.

'Who's she?'

Seren pulled her cap down. This one

hadn't been here before, but she recognised him. He was from the local paper, eager to get a scoop on his doorstep, and he was looking at her with the stirring of recognition. She'd always told her mother that one day she'd bleach her hair, or get purple contact lenses!

'Aren't you — '

'My personal slave,' Matt said. 'Now, report me to the authorities.'

Uncertain laughter rippled around them, just for a moment, but it had the desired effect of stopping the curious reporter in his tracks, unwilling to be found foolish in front of the hot shots from the big publications.

'Move it.'

Neither of them had ever thought they would be thankful to find Broken-nose bearing down on them.

'I've warned you lot. You've seen these two go in and out for months. Now, just back off, and let them through. One more stunt like this — '

He was waving his mobile in one

large paw, leaving the assembled reporters uncertain as to whether he intended
calling the local police, or less orthodox
reinforcements.

'OK, OK, only asking. Come on,
mate, we're just trying to do our jobs.'

'Farther back!'

He turned to Matt.

'Now, beat it,' he said, nodding his
head towards the entrance.

'At least we'll never have to do that
again,' Matt said feelingly.

★   ★   ★

For once, the day seemed to drag.
There was no point in starting anything
new, so it was just a matter of tidying
up, and loading up their tools into the
van, ready for their next garden, on
Monday.

'An ordinary garden will be a piece of
cake after this,' Matt remarked, as they
swept the dirt off the paths, and gave
the windows of the greenhouse a last
clean. 'Pity about the pineapples and

the melons, though. I wish we'd had time to get them started. Never mind, did Alun tell you Huw has arranged for us to come once a week to keep the place tidy?'

'Yes,' Seren replied, without enthusiasm. 'Although it shouldn't need both of us, if we get really busy with other work.'

'Oh, I don't know. They'd have had several men working full-time when this was created, and we can take on new staff, if we do get that busy. I'd like to see this through, see if we can persuade them to try the exotic fruit. Even get the National Trust involved.'

Seren smiled at the castles Matt was busily building in the air. Maybe he would not be quite so keen on returning here so often if Dylan and Chantrelle didn't renew their wedding vows, and what all that might lead to.

'Maybe,' she said.

By late afternoon, there was nothing more left to do, and the two went up to join Huw and Hefina for tea. Huw had muttered something about Chantrelle and Dylan joining them, but, much to Seren's relief, there was no sign of either.

'They had hoped to be here,' Huw said, looking faintly embarrassed at this sign of his employer's rudeness. 'I'm afraid Chantrelle has so much to organise with this party and photo shoot coming up, and Dylan was, ah, called away.'

That meant Huw hadn't a clue where he was, Seren thought to herself.

'Oh, that's fine. Don't worry. We know they are very busy people,' she said with a smile.

'But we all know how hard you have worked, and what a good job you have made. That garden is transformed. I never thought it would look like that again.'

'You wait until next year, Huw, when everything has had time to get established,' Matt said. 'Now that is when it will really look its best.'

'I'm sure,' Hefina said and gave a

144

slightly rueful smile. 'It's a pity Chantrelle can't wait until then for the photos to be taken. She's insisting on the next few weeks, when even the sweet peas won't be out properly.'

It seemed there was a particular urgency to Chantrelle's arrangements. Perhaps the reporters had been right this morning, after all. Maybe the two were about to renew their marriage vows.

'Maybe she can have them in, all over again.'

'Maybe,' Hefina said, although she did not sound at all sure.

'It'll be quiet without you and Matt here,' Huw said, joining Seren where she stood, quietly looking out of the window.

'It'll be strange not being here. It feels as if we have been here a lifetime, in the nicest possible way, of course.'

They smiled at each other.

'I hope you don't mind getting caught up in our little disagreements,' Huw said.

Seren looked up in surprise.

'Did we? I think everyone has been kind and helpful.'

'Chantrelle and Dylan, I mean.'

'Oh.'

Huw was looking at her, his eyes serious.

'You don't have to take their little squabbles too seriously, you know. They are both such passionate people, it often just happens like that. You know what artists are like, but they always make up. There's no doubt about it, they were made for each other.'

He sounded almost as if he was warning her. Seren looked at him. Did he think she was in some kind of danger?

'I'm sure,' she replied.

'Which is what this thing with restoring the garden has been all about, to last for ever.'

'Of course.'

It was just Huw being kind, she realised, gently warning her, making sure her heart did not get bruised in a lost cause. She smiled at him brightly, to let him know his suspicions were groundless.

'I'm glad we were able to help.'

All too soon, tea was over, and it was time for Matt and Seren to leave.

'I'll just check we've left nothing behind,' Seren called, as Hefina walked them to the van for the last time.

The two waved at her, and she set off down to the garden. She was quite certain they had left nothing, but she wanted just one last look around, on her own. The door was slightly open. She slipped through and just stood there. How much it had changed, and yet it was still the same. The abandoned feeling had not left it. Maybe when the flowers came, it would be better and people moved in and out, not that they ever would, she suddenly realised. Dylan and Chantrelle were hardly ever here, and Huw and his sister were so busy running the place, and their employers' concerns, that they would have little time for sitting here. All that work, she thought, gloomily, and they had not really brought the place to life at all.

'You look as if someone had died.'

The voice was close to her. She swung round, and found Dylan Jones sitting on a stone near the covered seat, open sketch book in his hand.

'Sorry, I didn't mean to startle you,' he said.

'I didn't see you!' Seren exclaimed. 'I thought you were off somewhere.'

'I was, but I came back early, and found no-one around.'

He smiled.

'I thought you wouldn't be able to resist coming back for one last look.'

'You mean, you were lying in wait for me?'

'Of course not. Just hoped to be able to say goodbye in a civilised manner. I'm not very good at the tea-party thing, I'm afraid. Not my style.'

Seren frowned at him.

'I'd better go,' she said. 'Matt will be waiting.'

'Not if he's got Hefina to keep him company,' Dylan returned, with a slightly wry smile.

Seren blinked. What did he know about that?

'Sit down, just for a moment. I need a figure on the seat. I just can't get the proportions right.'

'OK,' she said, unwilling, and she sat down as he began to sketch.

'I found out who that was, you know, in the old photograph.'

'Oh?'

'Yes, it wasn't my great-grandmother, after all, but her sister, my great-aunt Judith.'

He looked up with a smile.

'The black sheep of the family.'

'Never!'

Despite herself, Seren was intrigued.

'She didn't look at all black-sheepish in the photo.'

'Well, she was. I was always hearing about her when I was a kid. She fell in love with an engineer from the village, a working man, not at all the done thing.

The family did their best to stop her, but she wouldn't give him up. Said she couldn't live without him. In the end they eloped, and her name was never mentioned again.'

'How sad.'

Seren looked around her. The story seemed to fit the melancholy atmosphere of the place. To her surprise, Dylan was laughing.

'Sad? Not a bit of it. They made it to America, worked hard, and made a fortune. They ended up far richer than any of the family here. So, in the end, after my great-great grandfather died, some of the family started talking to her again. We're still close. I stay with her great-granddaughter when I'm in New York. In fact, I'm doing this picture for Judith, to show her, along with the photograph. You wait. She'll be over here in a shot. There, see what you think.'

He joined her on the seat, and held out the sketch for inspection. Her sense of gloom quite gone, Seren laughed as she viewed it. The figure on the bench was exactly the same pose as the one in the photograph. On the one hand she recognised herself, on the other . . .

'Dylan, how could you! I've never worn a bustle in my life.'

'I just couldn't resist it,' he replied, with a teasing smile. 'Besides, Judith will love it. You know what Americans are like about these things.'

'Oh, yes, and what happens when you explain to her that this is the gardener?'

'Is that what I tell her?' he replied.

There was something in his voice that made Seren look up quickly. He was sitting very close to her, and his eyes were on her face. There was an intensity in them that set her pulses racing.

'Seren,' he said, 'I so hoped you would come here. I must talk to you.'

'No.'

She pulled herself away, and stood up.

'Seren! Just hear me out, will you? I want to explain.'

'I don't want to hear,' she retorted, frowning. 'Especially not in this place. I don't want to play games.'

'A game? Is that what you think this is? I don't play games.'

'Neither do I. Enjoy renewing your vows with Chantrelle. I might even read the reports in the papers. I'm sure the photographs will be lovely.'

'Seren!'

'I have to go. I told Matt I'd only be a moment.'

He made a movement towards her, as if to grasp her arm, but she was too quick for him, and the next moment was running to where Matt and Hefina were waiting for her next to the van.

'Good riddance,' she muttered, as they shot through the pack of reporters for the last time. 'I hope I never have to go back there again.'

Matt looked at her from the corner of his eye, but made no comment. Something, it seemed, had happened to seriously upset her. She was sitting beside him struggling to keep back the tears.

'It will soon blow over,' he told himself, as the van shot down the winding road towards the village.

10

Seren yawned, settled herself comfortably in amongst the cushions of the window seat, and stretched. The autumn sunshine, flooding through the bay windows of the cottage, was warm, leaving her relaxed, and more than a little sleepy.

She would have to stop work soon. Her eyes were growing tired with a day of trying to capture the delicate lines of the orange lily before her. Engrossed, she had scarcely noticed that the rain had stopped, and the early-evening light made a walk along the cliffs look particularly inviting. Just this one last bit, she decided, before the flower faded, and lost its freshness.

She had always loved this part of Cornwall. It was where they had come as a family when Dad was still alive. She missed the mountains, of course, but there were the cliffs, and the small, rocky bays with their clear green water and pebbly beaches. They had been to this cottage more than once. It was still the same as she remembered, small, simply furnished, and with a garden stretching to the cliffs. There were no distractions, a good place to work, she had decided when she had booked the place. And about as far away from Haulfryn Castle, and its occupants, as you could get.

She had just left. Not even Huw knew where she was going. She hadn't been able to face him after that last day at the castle. She left him a scribbled note with an apology, and a hope they would meet up soon. Matt had been philosophical about her decision to take a break.

'Alun will find someone to fill in while you're away, no worries. You're right, it's a chance you've got to take. And it could lead to so much.'

So here she was, marooned in a cottage on the outskirts of a pretty

Cornish village, spending the last of the warm weather making the detailed illustrations for Alun's book. Everyone had been very kind. Several of the shopkeepers remembered the family who had stayed here so often. They had a vague recollection that Seren's mother was an artist of some kind, but that was all. Only the youngster from the florist looked at her strangely, as well he might, as he delivered the regular bunches of flowers to the cottage.

'You're popular,' he remarked, with undisguised curiosity, as the third bouquet in a week appeared at her door.

'Oh, it's work,' she replied, taking the envelope, which she knew contained detailed instructions from Alun. 'I'm illustrating a book on gardening.'

The young man did not look entirely convinced. He had obviously had a much racier explanation ready in his mind, but he made no further comment as he left.

She had worked hard, and there were now only a few of the drawings left to do. Then there was nothing for it but to go back home, back to her life again. She sighed, growing gloomy already at the thought. Still, there was no use in brooding. She shook herself, and looked out of the window once more. She could hear the waves crashing on the rocks outside.

It promised to be a beautiful evening, one too good to spend indoors. Maybe she would walk along the cliffs to the village, forget about cooking, and have a meal in the new restaurant by the harbour. It was time she came out of her solitude, and started to face the world again. She put down the drawing, and began to tidy her pens and pencils away.

Halfway through, she paused. There was no mistaking, it was a car, making its way down the drive. Well, it was at least two days since her last floral delivery from Alun, she thought. What on earth could he have in store for her this time? She put the last piece of paper in a folder, and went into the kitchen to fetch a vase. As she filled it, she heard the car stop, and a door bang.

'It's open,' she called, making her way back into the room as the doorbell rang. 'Come on in.'

She placed the vase ready on the table, and picked up the file of drawings to move them to safety on the old-fashioned dresser next to the bay window. She heard the front door open, and footsteps make their way towards her.

'What is it this time?' she called. 'Something exotic, I hope.'

Her eyes widened as a familiar figure stepped into the room.

'Oh, my goodness,' she breathed, as the precious drawings shot all over the floor. She hurriedly tried to collect them all together.

'Here, let me help you.'

'I'm fine. I can manage. What on earth are you doing here?'

'Giving you a heart attack, it seems,' he replied. 'So, who was it you were expecting?'

'The florist from Alun, for his book. Illustrations, remember? Not that it's any business of yours.'

'No.'

He held out the collection of illustrations he had retrieved.

'They're looking good,' he remarked. 'Alun will be pleased.'

'Thank you. Now go away, will you, Dylan? I'll kill Matt when I get back. I told him I didn't want anyone to know where I was.'

'It wasn't Matt, despite considerable attempts at bribery, corruption and arm twisting.'

'OK, Alun, then.'

There was no way she was going to see a funny side to this. The very person she had wanted to escape, the very last person she wanted to find her was right in front of her!

'Not Alun, either, I'm afraid. He's taking this responsible father thing very seriously. He was more interested in pistols at dawn, if you ask me.'

That nearly got her, but she was determined not to give in to a smile, and break her resolve.

'Who, then? No-one knows, except — '

She frowned at him. Her mother would never have told him. Seren hadn't explained everything, but enough for Rhianna to know Dylan Jones was the last person on earth her daughter would want to find her. She would never have told him, would she?

'Mam?'

'I had to see you, Seren, to explain things. Your mother just wants you to be happy. Look, I'll leave now, if you like. She only told me where you were on condition that I left when you told me to.'

He nodded towards her mobile.

'Check with her, if you want. Anyhow, Alun is probably in hot pursuit behind me, ready to horse-whip me if I get out of line.'

This time, the smile came, despite

her resolve. The vision of Alun charging down from the mountains on his white horse, ready for a duel to the death to protect her honour and happiness was too much.

'Don't talk nonsense,' she said. 'This is not Jane Austen, you know.'

'Well, I hope you tell Alun that, if he arrives.'

Seren laughed.

'OK. You've got five minutes, no more. Then I'm off to the pub.'

'Very ladylike, I'm sure.'

'Well, all right, the local restaurant, and, no, I don't need company, thank you. This is the twenty-first century, you know. I earn my own living, and I don't faint on demand. I can eat a meal in a public place without your help, thank you very much.'

'That's what I love about you,' he began, until her glare stopped him.

'And I don't mess with married men,' she said sharply. 'Someone always ends up getting hurt.'

'That's what I wanted to tell you.'

'That your wife doesn't understand you?'

'Not exactly.'

'Oh, don't tell me, you are not married,' she shot back with sarcasm.

'Well, yes.'

At the unexpected response, Seren found her mouth had dropped open. She shut it fast.

'I've been working for your wife for months, Dylan. Pull the other one.'

'Seren, don't you ever read the tabloids?'

'You know I don't.'

'Right. Wait here.'

He vanished, to reappear with a bundle of papers.

'I had a feeling you wouldn't be starting with the gossip pages now,' he said. 'But I thought you might have noticed one of the headlines.'

He spread out a collection of papers, all of which seemed to have Chantrelle staring out from the front page.

'If you'd taken a look at these, you

would know that Chantrelle and I are divorced.'

'Divorced?'

She looked at him, blankly. She didn't know much about divorce, but she had a feeling it couldn't just be done so quickly.

'I'm sorry,' she muttered feebly, feeling this was the right thing to say under the circumstances.

'Sorry? Sorry? My dear girl, have you any idea how long it has taken me to get Chantrelle to sign those papers?'

Seren found herself staring again.

'Oh, come on, Seren, it must have been obvious, even to you, that we weren't even on speaking terms those last few weeks.'

'But Huw said — '

'I bet he did,' Dylan replied darkly. 'Hasn't it ever occurred to you that Huw might have, shall we say, an ulterior motive, for wanting you to believe it was all wedded bliss?'

'But the garden — ' she protested.

'Ah, yes, the garden, the little flowery

love-nest to show the world just how happy we really are. I knew she was up to something, which was why I rushed back unannounced, before she could cover up her little scheme. Look, Seren, if my wife had presented a garden full of roses for our wedding anniversary in front of half the world's Press, how on earth do I turn round and start talking about divorce? I do have some pride, you know.'

'Oh.'

She looked at him. There were so many ideas whirling round her head, she didn't know where to begin.

'Sit,' he ordered.

'I'm not a dog!'

'Sorry. I'm not very good at this. Why don't I make us a cup of tea, and I'll start from the beginning.'

'I'll do it. You don't know where things are.'

'OK. I'll help you.'

They made the tea in silence, and returned to the window seat.

'How did I get myself into this mess?'

Dylan asked. 'I should have listened to Hefina, in the first place.'

Hefina! Seren had momentarily forgotten about her friend. Where did Hefina fit in all this, she wondered.

'Hefina?' she asked, tentatively.

'Yes. They were in the same class together, right the way through school. Hefina never had much time for her. I just assumed it was because she was so, well — '

'Pretty?'

'Er — yes. I was wrong, OK? I was young, headstrong, and not nearly as wise as I thought I was. I should have known Hefina would never be so petty. And anyhow, by the time Sian and I got together seriously, Hefina was working in London, following her glittering career.'

'Sian?'

Hefina had once mentioned a Sian.

'Chantrelle. You don't think she was born with that ridiculous name, do you? Chantrelle is her professional name. She was Sian when I met her.'

'Oh.'

Seren's head was in a whirl.

'We seemed to be on the same wavelength, going the same places, if you know what I mean, which meant getting out of Haulfryn and conquering the world, her with her modelling, me with my photography. It was a marriage made in heaven, for a few years, at least. Then we started going in different directions. She wanted more of the high life, I grew bored, impatient. All I wanted to do was to return to my painting and leave all the glitz behind, something Sian will never be able to understand. She was always afraid that if we split up she would lose her place in the limelight. Modelling is a pretty ruthless profession. There are always younger girls coming up through the ranks, ready to become the next big thing.'

'Poor Chantrelle,' Seren sighed.

'Oh, she'll be fine. She's a born survivor,' Dylan said drily. 'Why else do you think she finally agreed to give me my freedom?'

He picked up the first of the papers on the table.

'See what I mean?'

Seren looked at the picture closely for the first time.

'Why, that's Alex Rylance!' she exclaimed.

Chantrelle gazed out at her from the front page, glowing with beauty, beaming with happiness, while the headlines promised exclusive interviews about how she had found true love and fulfilment at last, and her plans for the future.

'She'll be picking up an Oscar in no time,' Dylan said, somewhat sourly. 'Just you see.'

'Well, if that's what makes her happy.'

'You're right, of course. I just don't appreciate being branded the husband from hell, that's all.'

'Oh, who cares? It'll be forgotten before you know it. You'll just have to work hard and prove otherwise, that's all.'

'Dear Seren.'

'I'm not your dear Seren.'

'Hasn't it occurred to you that I've come all this way to ask you to be?' he retorted impatiently.

'That's what I like about you, always so romantic. And so considerate of other people's feelings.'

'Ouch.'

He winced under the sting of her tone.

'I deserved that one. Look, Seren, can't we start again? No pressure. I'll leave, now. I know how important it is to you to finish these drawings, and I don't want to stop you. I owe you so much, inspiring me to start drawing again, to have the courage to do what I really want, and not what others expect of me. I was going slowly mad these past years, and you gave me back my sanity. I couldn't hurt you for the world.'

His voice was intense, but surprisingly gentle. Seren swallowed. She did not dare say a word, afraid that just the sound of her voice would give her away. He would know just how the fight had gone out of her, how she would never be able to pull herself away, or escape the strength of his arms. He seemed to take her silence as a sign of her desire to see him go. When he spoke again, there was a quiet sadness to his words.

'I just couldn't leave it like that, Seren, not having the chance to tell you how I felt, thinking you might meet someone, or that you might decide to stay here, and I'd never see you again. Please, will you at least promise me that you will come back, when you are ready? We can at least try to be friends, and then take it from there.'

'And Hefina?'

'Hefina? What about Hefina? She likes you. If you want to know, she misses having female company around the place.'

'But I — '

She faltered. She found him frowning at her.

169

'Seren! I hope you don't think what I think you are thinking,' he growled. 'Because if you are, forget it. I love Hefina dearly, but she's always been like a sister to me.'

He saw Seren going red with embarrassment, and deliberately lightened his tone.

'Hey, come on. Hefina has put up with my tempers ever since she was five years old. Don't you think she knows better than to let herself in for a lifetime of them? She made her mistakes in London. I don't know exactly what happened, but I know she was badly let down. I have a feeling it was one of her colleagues in the firm she was working for. All I know for sure is that she was close to a nervous breakdown when she came back to Haulfryn. It was the only reason she agreed to work with me at the castle for a while, to get back on her feet before she braved the bright lights again. Pity. She's the best at her job. Mind you, thanks to your friend,

Matt, she might just have a reason for staying on.'

Seren turned hastily to look out of the window again, anxious to hide the tears welling up in her eyes.

'Look,' she heard Dylan say behind her, 'I'll go. I don't want to upset you. I shouldn't have come. I just couldn't bear the thought of not seeing you, of not being able to explain myself. It's better you're away from it all, anyhow, until things die down. It's all very messy at the moment. You're best out of it. The Press is having a field day, and I know how you loath all that publicity. I just wanted to ask you to think things over, so that maybe, when this is all over, you might just consider — '

'Yes.'

He found she had turned to face him, tears trickling down her cheeks.

'Pardon?' he said, anxiously, feeling she had misunderstood him.

Then he saw that it was the broad smile on her face that had caused the tears to escape from the corners of her eyes, eyes that were sparkling with love and happiness.

'The answer's yes,' she said.

Her mother's mischief had entered her smile at the look of blank astonishment on his face.

'Unless, of course, you'd prefer to withdraw the question. I'll quite understand. I know the reality of these things.'

Alun and his pistols be damned! There was only one answer to that. All promises to behave impeccably forgotten, Dylan stepped forward, gathered her into his arms, and had silenced her in a moment. Given recent form, he half expected at least a kick on the shin for his pains, but Seren had no objections at all.

11

'Here we go!' Matt called, as, once again, the battered, old van made its way up to Haulfryn Castle.

The fresh sunshine of early summer danced on the waves below them, and set alight the ranks of multi-coloured blooms on either side of the steep, winding road up the cliffs.

'Ready?'

'As I'll ever be,' Seren returned, pulling the cap even closer over her eyes.

Outside the front gates, the large flock of reporters forced them to slow, almost stop.

'So, is it true?'

'No idea,' Matt called back, good humouredly.

'Is he getting married again?'

'Well, if he is, we're not likely to be invited, are we, now? I told you, we're the riff-raff.'

The nearest reporter looked through the windows at Matt's old jumper, and the grubby coat of his companion, and grunted with disappointment.

'It's only the gardeners again,' he remarked. 'So, you're sure you've not heard anything? I can make it worth your while.'

'I'll let you know,' Matt said.

This was all going better than expected. In fact so well, he could quite resist adding mischievously, 'So, how much?'

'Matt!' Seren hissed.

'Sorry, must go. Loads to do,' he called, arriving at the gate-house, thankful that they would now be free to make their way through into the safety of the castle grounds.

'Cameras.'

'I beg your pardon?'

Matt could not quite believe it! There was Broken-nose, glowering fiercely, motioning for them to wind down the window of the passenger seat. There was nothing for it. Seren opened the

174

window, allowing him to fit his head through the gap.

'Any cameras?' he demanded again, loudly.

'Er, no.'

Broken-nose was well aware that they were the very last people to be trying to smuggle in cameras. Matt wasn't sure if the guard had finally lost his marbles. If he had, then Matt did not fancy the task of having to do something about it, and those journalists would be too busy getting their pictures of the resulting mayhem back to head office first to lift a finger to help. Matt cleared his throat.

'Good.'

Broken-nose gave the interior of the van a quick inspection, finishing with his face not far from Seren's. All of a sudden, one eye closed slowly, in an unmistakable wink.

'Good luck, miss,' he muttered under his breath and the next moment he had vanished.

'Move on!' he was shouting. 'Oi! Watch it, you lot. What did I tell you!

One more stunt like that . . . '

As the van shot on its way, he was waving his arms, his menacing manner decidedly back up to speed. The occupants of the van simply looked at each other, and laughed.

As they came in sight of the castle, Matt stopped the van for a moment, and took out his mobile.

'No problems,' he announced. 'We're on our way.'

He dialled again.

'It was fine,' he said. 'There are about fifteen of them, but none too pushy.'

'Good, good,' came Alun's voice at the other end.

'If you hurry, you'll find the guard is keeping them more or less fully occupied.'

'Roger, over and out,' Alun replied, apparently taking this very seriously.

Matt turned to grin at his companion, who had taken the opportunity to step outside for a moment, and was removing the old coat and cap. She now stood there in a simple white gown.

'Why, you look beautiful, Miss Evans,' Matt approved.

'Thank you. My hair's a mess. I hope Hefina remembered her comb.'

'Calm down, Seren! There's bound to be something resembling a brush or a comb in that castle up there.'

Seren smiled, sat down again, and the van set off again, this time in a more leisurely manner.

'I still think I should be the one giving you away,' Matt said.

'And deprive Alun of his big moment to prove his conversion to a father figure? He'd never have forgiven you.'

'Poor Alun.'

Matt's eyes were twinkling.

'The end of a lifetime of chasing pretty women.'

'Well, he did have the choice,' Seren retorted.

'And I know he made the right one,' Matt said, as the van drew up in the carpark, where Hefina was waiting for them.

'Everyone's here,' she said, giving

Matt a quick kiss. 'I hope Dylan has settled down. He hasn't been able to stay still for a moment all morning. He's been prowling round the grounds like a bear with a sore head. He was quite sure you were going to think the better of it, and take off on a flight to Australia.'

'As if I would!' Seren exclaimed.

'That's what I told him, but you know Dylan. You'd better go and put him out of his misery,' she added to Matt. 'We'll be just five minutes putting the finishing touches.'

While Matt went off to join the others, Hefina quickly smoothed down Seren's dress, applied a brush to the hair ruffled by the disguising cap, and fixed a small veil carefully to her head.

'Huw didn't make it then,' Seren said.

'No, but he phoned this morning. Said to wish you luck. Don't worry about him. He'll come round in time. I think he just needs time on his own for a while. It will do him good, being away from here for a bit.'

'I didn't mean to hurt him, Hefina,' Seren said seriously.

'I know. And he'll see that, in time. These things happen.'

Hefina stood back to admire her handiwork.

'There you are. All done.'

'Are you sure? Does it look all right? It's not too plain, is it? I mean, I don't look at all — '

She stopped, panic rising.

'Like Chantrelle?'

'Well, yes.'

'Of course, you don't look like Sian. You're you.'

Hefina smiled, and gave her an affectionate kiss on the cheek, careful not to disturb her work.

'And I have a feeling, knowing Dylan, that was part of the attraction. And don't you ever forget it.'

Seren smiled at her. Dear Hefina. She could hear now the tone of easy affection when she referred to Dylan. How on earth had she ever convinced herself her friend was madly and hopelessly in love with her employer? All too easily, she reflected, beginning to blush. Fortunately, she was saved by the arrival of her mother and Alun.

'You got through all right?' Hefina called to them.

'No problems, apart from Rhianna attempting to convince them all she was Dylan's blushing bride.'

'Mama!'

'Oh, come on, darling, you wouldn't begrudge your mother a little fun, would you? They're always saying Dylan Jones has lost the plot. I just gave them a helping hand, that's all. Anyhow, you look beautiful. Your father would have been so proud.'

A few minutes later, Seren stood with Alun at the little garden gate, through which she had been so many times.

'Ready?'

Alun was looking very solemn. Seren nodded.

'By the way, the publishers rang just as we were leaving. They love the illustrations you did for my book. They were trying to contact you to talk about future projects.'

'Oh, Alun, that's wonderful!'

'I hope you don't mind, dear. I told them you were a little busy at present, but you'd get back to them in a few weeks. They were very understanding, given the circumstances.'

Alun pushed open the door, and the two stepped inside. Even though she had been working there only a short while before, helping with the preparations, the sight still took Seren's breath away. Everywhere she looked, growth glistened in the sunshine. New leaves uncurled on the fruit trees, and scarcely a patch of bare earth was to be seen.

Neat rows of vegetables lay on either side of the main paths, and the aroma of herbs filled the air. She walked slowly with Alun under a canopy of sprawling clematis, towards the central arbour, now almost hidden under the rampant growth of sweet peas, where their small group of friends was waiting.

'It's so beautiful,' she breathed, 'and so alive,' she added to herself. 'And for ever,' she vowed, as Dylan turned to greet her with his slow smile, and took her hand, to make her his wife.

THE END

We do hope that you have enjoyed reading this large print book.

Did you know that all of our titles are available for purchase?

We publish a wide range of high quality large print books including:
Romances, Mysteries, Classics
General Fiction
Non Fiction and Westerns

Special interest titles available in large print are:
The Little Oxford Dictionary
Music Book, Song Book
Hymn Book, Service Book

Also available from us courtesy of Oxford University Press:
Young Readers' Dictionary
(large print edition)
Young Readers' Thesaurus
(large print edition)

For further information or a free brochure, please contact us at:
Ulverscroft Large Print Books Ltd.,
The Green, Bradgate Road, Anstey,
Leicester, LE7 7FU, England.
Tel: (00 44) **0116 236 4325**
Fax: (00 44) **0116 234 0205**

Other titles in the
Linford Romance Library:

VISIONS OF THE HEART

Christine Briscomb

When property developer Connor Grant contracted Natalie Jensen to landscape the grounds of his large country house near Ashley in South Australia, she was ecstatic. But then she discovered he was acquiring — and ripping apart — great swathes of the town. Her own mother's house and the hall where the drama group met were two of his targets. Natalie was desperate to stop Connor's plans — but she also had to fight the powerful attraction flowing between them.

THE GYPSY'S RETURN

Sara Judge

After the death of her cruel father, Amy Keene's stepbrother and stepsister treated her just as badly. Amy had two friends, old Dr. Hilland and the washerwoman, Rosalind, with her fatherless child Becky. When Rosalind falls ill, Amy is entrusted with a letter to be given to Becky on her marriage. When the letter's contents are discovered, it causes Amy both mental and physical suffering and sets the seal of fate upon Rosalind's gypsy friend, Elias Jones.

WEB OF DECEIT

Margaret McDonagh

A good-looking man turned up on Louise's doorstep one day, introducing himself as Daniel Kinsella, an Australian friend of her brother-in-law, Greg. He said he had come to stay whilst he did some research — apparently Greg had written to her about it. Louise's initial reaction was to turn him away, but he was very persuasive. However, she was to discover that Daniel had bluffed his way into her life, and soon she found herself caught up in his dangerous mission.